A PLACE IN TIME

The Silver Sword

WRITTEN BY DEBRA JOY FINLEY
ILLUSTRATED BY TIFFANY JOY HINES

Order this book online at www.trafford.com
or email orders@trafford.com

Most Trafford titles are also available at major online book retailers.

This is a work of fiction. All the characters are fictitious and not based on any real people. The times and places in the book are based on actual events and locations.

Note for Librarians: A cataloguing record for this book is available from Library and Archives Canada at www.collectionscanada.ca/amicus/index-e.html

Printed in Victoria, BC, Canada.

ISBN: 978-1-4269-1655-7 (sc)

Our mission is to efficiently provide the world's finest, most comprehensive book publishing service, enabling every author to experience success. To find out how to publish your book, your way, and have it available worldwide, visit us online at www.trafford.com

Trafford rev. 9/2/2009

www.trafford.com

North America & international
toll-free: 1 888 232 4444 (USA & Canada)
phone: 250 383 6864 ♦ fax: 812 355 4082

THE SILVER SWORD

ALSO BY DEBRA JOY FINLEY

A PLACE IN TIME SERIES:

THE AMBER NECKLACE
THE SILVER SWORD

SOON TO BE PUBLISHED:
THE RED DIARY

To Ivan, the best knight a girl could ask for. Forever, Your Princess

THERE IS NO DEATH
ONLY A CHANGE OF WORLDS
CHIEF SEATTLE

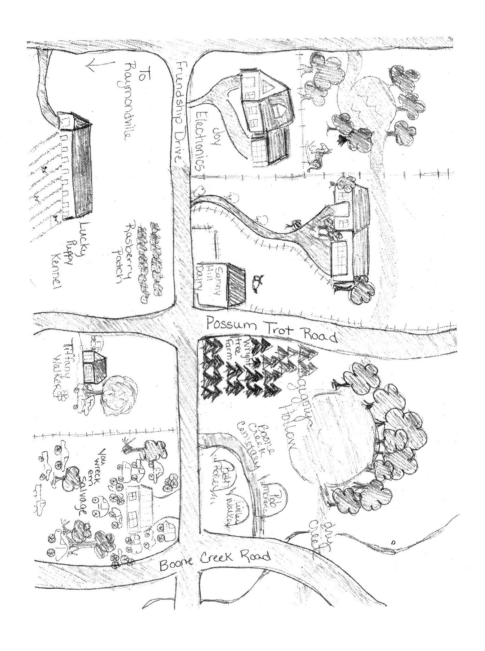

To Raymondville

Friendship Drive

Joy Electronics

Lucky Puppy Kennel

Rasberry Patch

Sunny Hill Dairy

Possum Trot Road

Tiffany Wickes

Wright Tree Farm

You wreck em salvage

Boone Creek Conservation

Guano Hollow

Betty Vaughn's House

Rio Vista

Boone Creek Road

PROLOGUE

Wilson Creek, Missouri
The Battle of Bloody Hill
August 10, 1861

"HAVE YA SEEN Rob McFarley? He rides a strawberry roan. She's a beaut, you'd 'member her." Nathan stood next to a huge cast iron kettle which hung over a crude campfire. The smell of boiling corn scented the air and made his stomach growl. He could almost taste the ripe kernels. The corn had been picked earlier from farmer Ray's field by hungry confederate soldiers who were camped nearby. They were fighting under General Sterling Price and hadn't had a good meal in days. Even though Nathan hadn't eaten yet today, he couldn't wait for the corn to finish cooking; he had to find Rob, his older brother.

A soldier, dressed in gray, standing with the help of a broken tree branch, answered his question. "Calvary you say? Went up that hill over yonder. By the sounds of things I think Johnny Reb has met the Yanks.

Nathan could hear the blast of heavy artillery and the booming of cannons. Pops and snaps from thousands of guns could be heard answering the challenge. Gray coats were running in all directions. How would he ever find Rob? Why did he run off and enlist? He was needed back home on the farm. Things weren't going so good back there, that's why Ma sent him off on foot to hike over fifty miles. It had taken him three days to complete the journey and he still hadn't found Rob. They were desperate for his help.

Back home, Nathan and Pa were harvesting the tobacco crop, plus tending to five milking cows, several head of beef and cutting hay. They were stretched pretty thin, but with Ma's help they were able to keep their heads above water-just barely. But then, a few days ago, a handful of Union soldiers galloped into the yard and forced Pa to join their army. They set fire to the tobacco field and hay stacks. They slaughtered the cows and steers. They trampled Ma's garden and even took the hams and sides of pork hanging in the smokehouse. Nothing of value was left for Nathan or his ma to eat or sell. They needed Rob's sharp wits and strong shoulders if they were going to save the farm. It was a good thing Rob was riding Cocoa, their prize-winning quarter house, or else the Yanks would have taken her too.

As Nathan's stomach rumbled in hunger, he watched soldiers mounted on swift horses gallop past him with their swords drawn, infantry marched in long columns across the cornfield with their rifles pointed forward. They were on the move up the hill to reinforce the troops caught in heavy fire.

Nathan saw a canteen hanging from a nearby tree branch and walked over to it. He unscrewed the lid and took a long drink of the warm water. He slung the canvas strap over his shoulder then started climbing the hill behind where the Calvary and infantry had made their camps. A thick layer of smoke hung over the battlefield. Nathan dropped down to his hands and knees and crawled to the crest of the ridge. Partially hidden by a thorny rose bush he watched the battle blaze before him. Losses were heavy on both sides. Wounded and dead soldiers lay everywhere.

As the sun reached its zenith in the blue sky, Nathan could finally see that the blue forces were turning away and running towards the North. With so many causalities the Confederates couldn't pursue the retreating Union soldiers. The ugly belching of the cannons fell silent. The pops from the rifles became fewer and fewer between, until a cease-fire was called.

On the smoke covered field, Nathan heard a sound worse than gunfire, the screams and cries of the wounded and dying under the hot noon sun. He had to find Rob among the thousands scattered across the hillside.

Nathan forced himself to move. His legs felt like lead as he walked around the bloody soldiers. He was becoming lightheaded from both the heat and the carnage before him. Nathan ignored pleas of help from the wounded, only straining his ears for one voice, that of his brother. His stomach felt hollow, his mouth was dry, which made it hard to swallow. Halfway down the bloody hill, Nick saw a cluster of hard woods off to his right. He turned and headed towards the haven of the trees. Just before reaching the welcome shade that the trees offered, the movement of a grazing horse caught his attention. It was a strawberry-roan!

Nathan raced over to the horse and recognized it to be Cocoa, their beautiful mare. Rob's saddle was still secured on her back. Searching the area around the horse, he found Rob. He was sitting propped against a boulder with his legs sticking straight out. His cap was tilted over his left ear and a bright red spot stained his uniform over his heart. Nathan dropped down on the grass and stared into Rob's glazed eyes looking for a sign of life.

"Rob! Rob!" He grabbed his brother's shoulders and shook him. "Talk to me. Oh, Rob." Nathan put his head on Rob's chest and embraced the cold corpse. He wept freely for the loss of this precious life. As the sun baked the battlefield, Nathan began to sweat heavily. He knew he had to return home and deliver the awful news to Ma.

Nathan closed his brother's eyes, straightened his cap, and folded his hands over his bloody chest. He picked up Rob's haversack from the ground, bowed his head, and said a quick prayer over his brother's body. Forcing himself to leave Rob's side, he turned and gathered up Cocoa's reins. Before mounting he talked softly to his brother's spirit. "I'll miss you, Bro. This war has robbed me of your life, maybe Pa's life too. Ma will loose the farm; everything will be lost. Some day this war will be over. Maybe then there will be a place in time when death doesn't have to shape one's destiny. I'll always love you, Rob."

Nathan bowed his head over his brother for the last time, swiped away the tears, and then quickly mounted cocoa. He turned for a final salute to the dead hero when the sun glinted off a shiny object. His eyes focused on the ground. Hidden by the tall grass he saw a silver sword lying next to Rob. He swung down and quickly picked up the weapon. He would carry Rob's silver sword back home and present it to their Ma.

CHAPTER ONE

Present Day
Raymondville, Missouri
Sunny Hill Dairy
August 6th

HE ROOSTER CROWED out in the yard, busy welcoming in another hot August day. Nick groaned, kicked the light blanket to the end of the bed, rolled over, and stared at the ceiling. The rooster crowed once again disturbing the silence of the morning. Nick sighed and swung his feet onto the worn wooden floor of the bedroom he was staying in at his aunt and uncle's house in the Ozarks. He sat on the edge of the bed cradling his head between his hands. As the mental cobwebs of the night gradually receded, Nick thought back to the events which led him to living in the Ozarks, a long way from Chicago.

Just over two months ago, on a rainy night in June, Nick's dad was forced off the road by a drunk driver. The ambulance responded in a timely manner, but they were too late to save his dad; his injuries were fatal. Not only did Nick lose his dad on that rainy night, but his dreams of leaving for college in the fall had died too. His dad was the sole breadwinner of the family and he didn't leave them with any life insurance, only bills, and a very small savings. Mom said she couldn't afford to send him to college. In fact, they couldn't even afford to stay in their small apartment anymore. When the lease expired in early August they were going to have to move into his grandparent's place. It was just a small apartment and he was going to have to share a room with his mother.

In four days, August 10th, Nick was going to turn eighteen. He couldn't imagine having to share a room with his mother. Fortunately, his dad's brother and wife, Uncle Joe and Aunt Sara, owned a dairy farm in Raymondville, Missouri. They were short-handed due to the death of their only son, Bobbie, last summer. They really needed an extra hand and could use Nick's help with the daily chores. Uncle Joe said that Nick was welcome to live with them for as long as he wanted. Nick didn't have any desire to milk cows, shovel manure, or sling hay bales around. But he just couldn't live with his grandparents, sharing a room with his mother, either. For now, his desire of becoming a computer engineer was going to be put on a back burner. Nick raised his head, rubbed the sleep from his eyes, and slowly rose to a standing position.

Nick really didn't miss living in Chicago. He had a few friends, but they were more interested in kissing girls, and drinking beer under the docks by Lake Michigan, than educating themselves for the future. However, Nick had dreams. He had just graduated from high school in May, and he desperately wanted to attend college. He wanted to learn everything thing there was to learn about computers so he could create his own game software and become rich, well, if not rich, to at least make enough money to support himself.

Nick owned a driver's license, but didn't have money to buy himself a car. It was part of his dream to have his own set of wheels. Living in the city he rode his 10-speed-bike just about everywhere. He had to leave his bike at his grandparent's place because all he could carry on the train was two suitcases filled with the clothes he would need living on the farm. He had boxed up his stereo and CD collection, left behind his roller blades, basketball, and Xbox games. His mom said Aunt Sara watches soaps all day and Uncle Joe watches talk shows in the evening. There would be no time for him to use the TV for his games. He felt shriveled inside, like a leaf that had fallen, shrunk, dried, and crumbled before the wind.

"Nicky. Come eat your pancakes." Aunt Sara banged on a cast iron skillet with a metal flipper. He was sure she'd wake the neighbors. Then, he remembered that the nearest neighbors were miles away. Sunny Hill Dairy was located on the corner of Friendship Drive, and Possum Trot Road; you could set off a cherry bomb and not wake your neighbor.

Nick tucked the T-shirt into his jeans and pulled his belt tight. He noticed he had lost some weight as he tightened the belt another notch. He wasn't fat, but a few pounds of weight loss actually made him look trimmer. He combed his short black hair off to the side, and slipped his feet into a pair of flip-flops. Before leaving the room he touched his dad's pocket-watch that was sitting on top of a brown dresser. The watch had been passed down from his grandpa and it was now time for Nick to own it. The watch had been broken in the accident and would never keep time anymore, but it was the only thing of his dads that he had kept.

"Hurry, Nicky. Uncle Joe is out bringing in the cows. He wants you to help milk this morning." Aunt Sara scooped up six pancakes and plopped them on his plate.

Entering the kitchen, Nick was amazed at the amount of food on his plate. "I can't eat six pancakes Aunt Sara, three would be just fine." Nick stared at the pancakes wondering if he could even swallow one. Instead of trying to eat, he grabbed the glass of milk sitting in front of his place setting and took a long drink. The milk was rich and creamy, not like the watery stuff his mom had always bought so it wouldn't clog your arteries. A lot of good that did for Dad. He had died with clean arteries, but no life insurance, and no college money.

"I'm sorry, Aunt Sara, but I can't eat anything this morning." Nick wiped away his milk mustache onto the back of his hand. "I'll just head out and help Uncle Joe with the cows or something."

"In those sandals? Your toes would be mashed to a pulp in no time. You wear those work boots by the door. They look to be your size." Aunt Sara turned off the fire under the skillet, which was still cooking a batch of pancakes.

There was no arguing with Aunt Sara. He went back to his room for a pair of socks, and then slipped into the worn boots. They were a perfect fit.

"Those were Bobbie's boots. I thought you'd need a pair, so I dug those out of his closet. Bobbie would have wanted you to have them." Aunt Sara lowered her head and turned away. She flipped the uneaten pancakes onto a nearby serving platter.

Nick had remembered his mom telling him about Bobbie's death last summer. He seemed to recall that it was some kind of freak farm accident. Bobbie was two years older than him, so he would have been around twenty. He was always showing fair animals. Aunt Sara would send them newsclippings of Bobbie holding onto a mean looking bull with one hand and in the other a blue ribbon. Uncle Joe and Aunt Sara were hoping to pass the farm on to their only son, but death stole that dream from them. Now here he was wearing Bobbie's boots and not liking it one bit. He had his dad's broken watch and Bobbie's worn boots. He was a real collector of dead men's things.

Nick closed the back door and slipped into the dim morning light. This was his first morning on the farm and he was unsure of what was expected of him.   Slowly, he walked to the first barn he could barley see in the dim light and stepped inside the open door.   It was dark inside and it smelled of fresh hay, ripe from the sun.   He walked further into the barn trying to make out the shapes before him.   A faint smell of manure mingled with the hay. He took a step forward and felt his boot land on a hard object.   He knelt down and felt for it under the sole of his boot.   His fingers touched a cold lump of steel.   He picked it up and stepped back to the door where it was lighter to see what he had found.

But, before he could open his hand, he started to feel light-headed and nauseous.   His legs felt like they were turning to jelly and he crumpled to the dirt floor.   Suddenly, he thought he saw a boy about thirteen years old dressed in homespun brown pants.   He wore a pair of suspenders over a cotton beige shirt.   He stood by the side of a dirt road busy peeling an apple with a pocketknife.   The knife had slipped and the boy had nicked his fingers on his right hand.   Nick watched as the boy dropped the apple to suck the wound.

The vision faded as Nick rapidly blinked his eyes and shook his head. Nick opened his fingers exposing the object lying on his palm.   It was a pocketknife and his hand was sticky with blood.

Chapter Two

ICK DROPPED THE knife and stared at his hand. He wiped the blood off onto his jeans. He didn't see any wound, nor did he feel any pain. He reached down for the knife and examined it carefully. He tried pulling out the blade, but it was rusted shut. It looked like a piece of junk, and he was about to throw it back into the darkness, when his fingers slid over a raised letter. He looked closer and saw that the knife was stamped with a large raised C. He slipped it into a front pocket of his jeans. He would ask Uncle Joe about it. Nick remembered Aunt Sara had said that the cows were waiting. Feeling better, he hurried to his feet and walked down to the next barn where he saw a light shinning through a flyspecked window.

He entered the milk house and saw a large stainless-steel tank sitting in the middle of the room. Two silver wash vats and a hand sink dominated the far wall. The compressor, cooling the bulk tank, was making quite a racket. He put his hands over his ears, and hurried over to the door across the room, that lead to the parlor.

Eight Holstein cows were being milked. They stood on two raised cement platforms; one on each side of a parlor. Four cows could be milked on each side simultaneously. Uncle Joe operated from between these two platforms, in a pit, which was about four feet lower than the platform the cows stood on. This made him about waist high to the cows, which was the perfect height needed to reach the eight, swollen, pink udders. As Nick entered, Uncle Joe was busy attaching the milking claws to the side of cows which had just entered. The claw automatically pulled the milk from the udders. The milk then flowed into a stainless steel pipe, which carried it to the bulk tank for cooling.

"Come on down here, Nick. You're late." Uncle Joe turned his attention to the other side of the parlor where the cows were just finishing up. He gently took one claw off a collapsed udder. "These cows are done. Take that milker off."

Nick gingerly stepped down into the parlor, being careful not to slip on the steep, damp cement steps. Once down in the pit, he looked up at the milking cows. The Holsteins looked huge from this perspective. Trying to please his uncle, Nick stepped close to a cow's hind leg and gingerly grabbed the metal milking claw which had just finished milking the cow. He turned off the plastic valve like he saw his Uncle do and the milker fell off, and onto his hand. He hung it up on a metal hook located next to the cow's hind leg.

"What did you do to your hand? Are you bleeding?" His Uncle took off two more milking claws, then opened the front gate to release the cows.

"Nah. I found this knife up in the first barn I came to. It had blood on it." Nick dug into his front pocket, and pulled out the rusty knife for him to see.

"That knife doesn't have blood on it. You cut yourself on the blade, didn't you? You best be more careful around the farm." Uncle Joe slammed the gate closed behind the exiting cows. The clanging metal echoed in the parlor.

"Do you know whose knife this is? I found it in the barn on top of the hill." Nick repeated himself and handed his uncle the knife.

"That's the hay barn ya talking about, and no, I've never seen this knife before. But look, see this raised C? The Confederate Calvary used to mark all their goods with a C. This could be a real find. Clean it up and you've got yourself a treasure." Uncle Joe handed Nick back the knife.

When Nick's fingers came in contact with the rusty steel, he once again saw an image of the boy who had cut himself. His hand was wrapped in a dirty rag and he was walking down a dirt road leading a strawberry-roan mare; his head was bowed under the hot sun. A silver sword hung down by his side. Nick blinked; then coughed. The vision disappeared, but he noticed that his hand was sticky with blood again.

He turned away from his uncle and shoved the knife into his pocket, planning to dispose of it as soon as possible. He rubbed the blood stain on his pants, trying to make it fade into the material. He didn't want his uncle to think he had cut himself again. Quickly, he stepped outside and moved four more cows into the parlor to be milked.

Uncle Joe instructed Nick how to wash off the cows' teats, check for mastitis, spray iodine on them afterwards to prevent infection, and stay away from kicking hooves and swatting tails. It was more than he ever wanted to learn about cows.

As the sun rose, the cows kept coming in from the holding pen, four at a time, until Nick's arms were sore, and he was spotted in specks of manure. As they milked his uncle talked.

"Sure wish I could have been there for ya when your dad died, Nick. Aunt Sara and I can't leave the cows to milk themselves ya know. You and Bobbie are a lot alike. He loved his cows. Bobbie was going to show Elmer in the August livestock show this year. He was proud of Elmer. Wait till you meet him; now there's a bull with personality. He'll be three this year, just entering his prime. I know I should have shot him after what he did to Bobbie, but I don't think Bobbie would have wanted that." Uncle Joe went quiet for a bit and even though Nick wanted to ask questions about Bob's death, he thought it would be best to change the subject.

"Any neighbors live close by?"

"Neighbors? Some new folks bought the old Joi Dairy place over on Friendship Drive, back in June. You might know them, heard they're from Chicago. A young lady around fifteen and her dad live there. She almost drowned in the Current River a few weeks back. These city folks, ha, they think the creeks down here are just a pretty water park. Anyways, he's opened up an electronic business and works out of his home. Interesting folk."

Nicks ears perked up at the mention of electronics. "Maybe I can get a job helping him?"

"You've got a job right here, son. Help me. I need you to milk cows. Don't worry. I'll pay ya good."

"Right, Uncle Joe." Nick couldn't see milking cows for the rest of his life, but they were giving him a roof over his head for the time being. How could his uncle like this job? It was a disgusting way to make a living. Finally, the last cow sashayed over the metal grates and out the door. But, he was soon to find out that the work didn't stop there.

His uncle showed him how to use the pressure-washer to hose down the parlor. "After you're done with that job, I need you to feed the calves. Then, ya have to walk down to the valley and check on Daisy. She's due to calve today. We need to keep a sharp eye on her."

"How will I know it's her?" Nick had no idea what a pregnant cow would look like.

"She's a Brown Swiss, so she's a light brown. Not dark brown, that's a Jersey, I mean real light brown, with a huge tummy." Uncle Joe laughed at his description.

Nick hosed the manure off the walls and floor, washing it down the drain. The parlor looked pretty good when he was done and he felt a touch of pride in his work. Of course his pants and left boot had gotten soaked when he lost control of the hose for a second, but he wouldn't let that happen again. He figured he'd get a lot of practice at this job.

After feeding the calves, Nick squished his way up the drive, walking by the hay barn and house. He followed a worn path leading into a valley nestled between thick woods. The cows were grouped by a small pond that was covered by a green slime. Nick remembered the rusty knife and pulled it from his pocket. Quickly, he tossed it into the middle of the pond. Its weight disturbed the slime, causing ripples to form on the surface in ever widening circles. Carefully, Nick studied the bunch of cows looking for Daisy, the Brown Swiss with a large tummy. But, all he saw were the black and white spotted Holsteins and a few dark brown cows. Those must be the Jerseys.

Nick had to widen his search. He strolled around the little valley, and peered into the dark woods. Finally, half hidden in the tall grasses he saw a cow lying on her side. She was light brown, just like Uncle Joe said, and her stomach looked ready to pop. Her tongue was hanging out the side of her mouth and was covered by white foam. Her eyes were rolled back and she moaned softly. Her belly cramped causing her legs to stiffen with her efforts.

"Hi, Daisy. Easy, girl." Nick walked around the cow to see what was happening under the tail. A little brown face, snuggled between two long legs, protruded from the birth canal. Two large black eyes, framed by long lashes, watched him. The calf's nose was dark brown and it wrinkled as if it were trying to smell its new environment. But, as hard as Daisy was pushing, the calf wasn't making any progress. Nick felt the calf didn't have long to live if it wasn't pushed out of the birth canal real soon. Its protective birth sack had broken and it couldn't breath. He didn't have time to run for Uncle Joe. He would have to do this himself.

"Don't worry, little girl. I won't let you die." Gingerly, Nick grabbed the two soft hooves with both his hands and pulled gently. The calf didn't budge. "Come out. Please, come out." Nick sat down on the grass, which was covered with morning dew, and braced his feet against the cow's rump.

Using more force, he tried pulling once more. The cow moaned in pain and strained for all she was worth. The calf began to slide forward. Nick adjusted his grip on the fore-legs, which were covered with slick mucus, and pulled in time to Daisy's contractions. Like a cork from a bottle, the calf popped free and landed on Nick's lap.

"We did it!" Nick shouted as he squirmed out from underneath the wet calf. Blood and birth fluids covered his jeans, shirt, and arms. It smelled fresh, like when it first starts to rain, but it was very sticky.

Daisy heaved herself to her feet and began licking the newborn. Nick scooted back to give Daisy some room. With a goofy smile on his face he watched the antics of the calf. First, it sneezed and uttered a loud moo. Then, it rose up onto a pair of shaky legs. Soon, it butted its little nose against mom's inner leg searching for the udder and a tasty treat.

After making sure both the new mommy and calf were going to be okay, Nick slowly rose to his feet, being careful not to startle them. Not wanting to take his eyes off the miracle of birth, he walked backward, and tripped over a rock. He fell and landed on his butt. Sitting on the ground, he saw an object just off to the side of him buried in the tall wet grasses. Rising to his knees, he used his fingers to pry the gray lump free. It was a canteen. The metal was dented, but the leather strap was still strong. He turned it over and saw a large, raised C stamped onto the metal.

CHAPTER THREE

 ALVARY! THE CANTEEN must be from the Civil War. At least this relic didn't make his hand bloody, or make him see weird things. He turned the canteen over and over in his dirty, stained hands. He could hear a sloshing on the inside. Curious as to what was making the noise, he unscrewed the cap and tilted the canteen downward. A stream of clear water trickled out. He dribbled it over his fingers. When the warm water made contact with his skin, the tranquil valley transformed into a battlefield of misery. Hundreds of soldiers were suffering, crying for a drink. A few soldiers were missing legs; some had an arm missing. Nick noticed a few men suffering from head wounds, while still others had been gut shot. "Water…Water…"

Nick dropped the canteen like it was a hot ember. He looked across the valley and saw Daisy and the calf, nothing else. He nudged the canteen with the toe of his work boot. Nothing happened. He touched the raised C stamped on the front with an extended finger, but his world stayed the same. Carefully, tipping the container over, he tried to encourage more water to come out. But it was all gone; nothing was left but a few drops, which dripped onto the grass. He shook his head, then picked up the canteen by its canvas strap and walked over to the woods. He hung the canteen on the nearest tree branch. This was another antique he wanted nothing to do with. He turned away from the tree and hurried across the fields, back to the barns, where he last saw his uncle. He was excited to share the news about Daisy and the newborn calf.

Uncle Joe was driving a 1030 Case tractor. He was pulling an empty feed-wagon out of the cow pasture. He had just finished filling the ten cement feed bunks with grain for the milk cows. Uncle Joe parked the tractor in the commodity shed, hopped down and met Nick, who was walking down the drive towards him.

"Daisy had a baby girl," Nick shouted. "She's a perfect, light brown calf. I even helped deliver her. It was awesome watching the calf arrive." Nick fell in step beside his uncle.

"You want her?" Uncle Joe slapped his cap along side his leg shaking off the grain dust.

"Want her? What do you mean, want her?"

"The calf's yours if you want to feed and care for her."

"Mine? Daisy's calf? You bet I want her." Nick couldn't believe he cared so deeply about a farm animal. Delivering the calf had helped him to understand why his uncle loved his animals.

"You feed her right and she'll be in the milking string three years from now. What's her name?" Uncle Joe was heading towards the house.

"I'd like to name her Rose. My mom loves roses. But, I can't promise you that I'll be here in three years from now."

"That's fine, son. We'll take it one day at a time. Rose is a fine name for your first calf. Tonight, we'll milk Daisy and you can bottle feed the milk to Rose. Now, let's wash up for dinner. How on earth did you get so dirty? Aunt Sara better wash that set of clothes; you're a mess."

Having had skipped a big breakfast, Nick was famished. Lucky for him, Aunt Sara had cooked up a storm: meatloaf, mashed potatoes, green beans, and chocolate cake for dessert. Nick washed it all down with a tall glass of fresh milk. As they ate Aunt Sara had a chance to question Nick.

"Do you need anything, Nicky? When we picked you up at the train station you only had two suitcases. If you need some work clothes, and you think Bobbie may have had it, you're welcome to anything in his room. I haven't had the heart to give any of his things away. I know someday I'll have to clean out his room but I just can't do it yet. Guess I'm still hoping he'll walk through that door again."

A lump formed in Nick's throat. He knew what Aunt Sara meant. He was still waiting for his dad to come home and toss his keys on the kitchen counter.

"Are you planning on going to college, dear?"

"I had planned on going to Northwestern University in Chicago this fall, but Dad dying changed all that."

"You can still go to college. What do you want to study?"

"I'm interested in computers, but now it looks like I need to learn about raising calves."

"Don't give up on your dreams so quickly, Nicky. Drury University holds classes in Cabool. That's only a thirty minute drive from here."

"But I don't have a car or any money for classes. It's hopeless." Nick pushed himself away from the table and stood. "May I be excused?"

"Of course you may, dear. Your uncle and I have an appointment in town this afternoon. You're free till chore time which is five o'clock, don't be late!"

Nick walked to his room and flopped down on the bed. A full stomach, combined with fresh air and chores, had him asleep in minutes. When he woke two hours later the house was quiet. His aunt and uncle must still be in town. Nick got up and walked down the polished hardwood floors to the closed door of Bobbie's room. He opened the door and stepped inside. The room looked like Bobbie had just slipped out for a minute. The bed was made and the sun streamed into the room, casting its warm glow over all of Bobbie's belongings.

Nick's eyes roamed around the room, but stopped at the desk where a computer sat. He quickly walked over to it and pressed the ON button. The computer booted itself up and displayed the files. Nick saw the icons for a few games, notes on various livestock, and a word processor complete with spell check. Nick had everything available he needed right at his fingertips. Now, all he needed was some college classes. He clicked off the computer and continued looking around.

There was one shelf of trophies. Another shelf was full of books on breeding and animal health. Nick was losing interest in Bobbie's belongings, when something shiny wedged between two floorboards caught his eyes. He bent over and carefully pried it from the crack. It was a metal button. He turned the button over and saw a raised C stamped on the face.

CHAPTER FOUR

 O. THIS CAN'T be happening here too." Nick moaned as his eyesight blurred. He thought he saw a soldier dressed in a clean, pressed, gray uniform standing tall and holding a silver sword. This soldier looked familiar to him. He had similar features to the boy that Nick had seen in an earlier vision; the boy who had cut his finger. Maybe this guy was his older brother!

Nick blinked and the image changed. Now the solider was slumped against a boulder. His uniform was ripped, buttons were missing, and a red stain had formed over his heart. The soldier's eyes had a glazed look to them. His silver sword lay in the grass beside him.

"Nicky. We're home." Nick jumped at his aunt's voice, dropping the button. It rolled back into the crack in the floor. The strange images faded and Bobbie's room came back into focus.

"It's five o'clock and chore time, Nick. Meet you in the barn." Down the hall he heard his Uncle Joe changing into his coveralls and work boots. Nick's hands were shaky and he felt lightheaded. He sat down on the edge of Bobbie's bed. He couldn't understand why he kept seeing scenes from the Civil War. Maybe, his dad's death had affected him more than he had thought. He wanted to talk to someone about this, but he didn't dare say anything to Uncle Joe. He'd think he was losing his marbles. If he talked to his mom, she would insist he come back to Chicago and live with his grandparents, where she could keep an eye on him. He didn't want to leave the farm. He felt needed here. Even if he did see dead soldiers, it was better than being cooped up living with two old people and sharing a room with his mom.

Nick slipped out of Bobbie's room and tiptoed back to his own room. He didn't want to run into his aunt or uncle just yet. The vision was still fresh in his mind and he was having trouble collecting his thoughts. He eyed the pile of dirty jeans and T-shirt on the floor that he had worn earlier. But, he just couldn't bring himself to wear them again. They were sticky with birthing fluids and dried manure. Looking through his drawers, he found a clean pair of jeans and a dark blue T-shirt. He quickly changed and joined his uncle out in the milk house.

The afternoon chores went smoothly. The cows didn't look quite so large to Nick this time. He was even starting to identify the different breeds his uncle owned. The black and white ones were Holsteins. The Jerseys were smaller, quicker on their feet, and dark brown in color. The light brown cows were the Brown Swiss. Now he just needed to learn all their names. After Uncle Joe milked Daisy, Nick took her milk from the treated bucket and poured it into a feeding bottle for Rose. Earlier, Uncle Joe had brought Rose in from the field and placed her into a calf pen, located in the hay barn. Nick now knew that hay bales were stored upstairs in the loft, and the bottom floor was divided up into small calf pens. At the end of the barn was one big pen made out of heavy beams and boards. That was where Elmer lived.

After feeding Rose her bottle, Nick strolled over to the large pen to have a look at Bobbie's "prize-winning-bull". A huge, dark-brown animal snorted at him through the boards. Nick jumped back, not wanting to be to close to that mean looking animal.

"You chicken?" A skinny boy was sitting in the shadows. He was perched on the top board of the pen and was chewing on a stem of hay. Nick came closer and noticed the boy's eyes which were sunken into a face that looked rather waxy and gray. Pieces of hay stuck out of his blond hair making it look like he hadn't combed it in weeks. His fingernails were cracked and dirty. His jeans were threadbare and his knees poked through the faded material.

"Where'd you come from?" Nick's heart was thundering in his chest like a runaway train.

"I'm your neighbor, Rob McFarley. You must be Cousin Nick, the city slicker from the North. This here is Elmer." He waved a bony hand towards the bull.

"So you know Elmer?" Nick moved in closer to see the famous bull.

"Yup. You going to show him Saturday at the big livestock show in Houston?"

"Me? I've never shown a bull before." Elmer strolled across the pen over to Nick. He shoved his big head forward, through the slats, looking for a scratch. Nick stuck his hands through the boards and rubbed his neck. "You mentioned Houston? Is that Houston, Missouri, or Houston, Texas?"

"Missouri, of course. It's the next town over, only about eight miles from here." Rob answered. "Slip Elmer's halter on over his ears and walk him around the pen." Rob kept chewing the piece of hay while giving free advice to Nick.

Nick took down a dusty halter hanging from a nail beside the pen and climbed over the boards. He slipped the halter over Elmer's furry head. The bull didn't seem to mind the attention and stood still while Nick fiddled around adjusting the buckles and straps.

"Here's a rope. Clip it under the chin where that metal ring is." Rob extended a rather frayed rope towards Nick, being careful not to leave his ring-side seat on the top board.

Nick clipped on the lead rope and gave it a tug. Elmer took a few steps forward and followed Nick. After about ten steps, Elmer, put his head down, gave a buck and a snort, and took off full-speed around the pen. Nick was jerked off his feet and dragged belly down in the manure- packed pen.

"Let go of the rope!" Rob shouted at Nick, who finally did release his grip. Catching his breath, Nick stood uncertain on shaky legs. He tried to brush off some of the manure which stuck to his jeans and shirt. So much for that clean outfit.

"Boy, you look a sight." Rob laughed and slapped his palm on his thigh. "You did real good for your first attempt. Try again."

Nick threw a dirty look at Rob and climbed out of the pen.

"Hey, where you going, *Yank*? The show's in four days, August 10th. Get back to work."

"Who said I was going to show Elmer?" Nick rubbed his bruised elbow. "And don't call me Yank. The war's long over."

"I'll ignore your sarcastic tone, *Yank,* and share with you the best part. How do you feel about winning 5,000 dollars in cold, hard cash?"

"5,000 prize money? You've got my attention. What do I have to do to win?" Nick wasn't sure he liked this strange boy, but he was willing to set aside his feelings and bruised limbs to learn more about the money. He stopped rubbing his sore elbow and listened closely to what Rob had to say.

"Elmer's got first class breeding. Bobbie knew he was a champion when he bought him as a baby, three years ago. All you have to do is make him lead, so you can show him in the ring. Elmer's fine lines will win you the prize." Rob jumped down into the pen next to Elmer. "Maybe we both can hold him."

Working together Nick and Rob forced Elmer to walk in circles until he was ready to settle down and be led. It looked like he was starting to remember his past training. Maybe this wouldn't be so hard after all.

"Before he died, Bobbie had Elmer trained to walk like a puppy, but in the past year, no one has really worked with him. He just needs a little love and affection. He'll polish up just fine." Rob unsnapped the lead rope and gave Elmer a pat on his shoulder, disturbing a layer of dust and dirt. "Phew, looks like Elmer needs a good bath. Come to think of it, so do you, *Yank*. You have about the same amount of manure on your clothes as he has on his fur."

Nick didn't care about his clothes right now; he was too excited about the show. "Think we can get him ready in time?"

"Yeah, I think he'll be ready."

"By the way, how exactly did Bobbie die?" Nick pulled Elmer's halter off, climbed out of the pen, and hung it back on the nearby nail.

"Elmer killed him."

"What?" Nick froze in his tracks.

"See, it's like this. Bobbie bent over to put grain in Elmer's bucket. Elmer butted him from behind, which threw Bobbie forward making him hit his head on that hay manger." Rob pointed to a wooden box nailed onto the stained boards. "Bobbie broke his neck when he hit. It was a freak accident if you ask me. Elmer was just playing. He didn't mean to kill Bobbie. That's why your Uncle Joe didn't have the heart to shoot Elmer, even though he was pretty broken up over loosing Bobbie." Rob pointed his index finger and raised thumb at Elmer's head. He lowered the thumb like he was shooting a make believe gun. "Hey, I've got to run. I'll be back tomorrow to help you some more."

"Thanks, *Reb*." Nick called over his shoulder. Rob smiled and saluted Nick before disappearing out the door. Nick hung around Elmer's pen a while longer. While he filled the hay manger with fresh hay and changed the water in the bucket, he talked softly to the bull. The whole time, Nick was careful not to bend over in front of Elmer. When he was finally done, Nick took Rose's empty bottle back to the milk house where Uncle Joe was just finishing up.

"Good Golly! How did you get so filthy feeding a calf? Your Aunt Sara isn't going to be very happy with you. Glad I'm not in your shoes."

Choosing to ignore this comment, Nick asked, "You know a Rob McFarley? I just met him in the hay barn back by Elmer's pen. He helped me lead Elmer around."

"You led Elmer, son? I'm real proud of you. You gonna try and show him on Saturday?"

"Yup. Rob said there's 5,000 in prize money."

"It's more than the money, Nick. If Elmer wins, you'll have yourself a top-notch bull, one with fine breeding lines."

Nick was learning that there was more to this farming business than just milk and manure. "I'm going to give it my best shot, Uncle Joe. With Rob's help, Elmer will be in top form. You know Rob?"

"Rob McFarley, you say?" He took off his John Deere cap and scratched his head. "The only McFarley's I know around here are all buried in the Boone Creek Cemetery."

CHAPTER FIVE

HAT DO YOU mean by, *buried in the cemetery?*" Nick turned and rinsed out Rose's empty bottle of milk with hot water. He set it on end to dry.

"Dead, son. The McFarley's lost most their kin in the Civil War, a terrible tragedy it was. There're all buried at Boone Creek Cemetery, except for the oldest boy. I heard that he's buried at Wilson Creek were he died fighting in the battle of *Bloody Hill.*"

"Must be a different Rob McFarley, cause the Rob I met lives some where close by. Maybe he's visiting some friends or something. Anyways, I can sure use his help. He's pretty good with Elmer and can give me some pointers."

"Well, Nick, you can use all the help you can get. Bet you didn't dream you'd be working with a bull just one week ago, did you?" Uncle Joe put his arm around Nick's shoulder, turned off the lights, and shut the door. "Let's call it a night." Together they walked up to the house. Nick enjoyed his uncle's heavy hand resting on his shoulder. Somehow, it made him feel less alone.

After spending a long time under the shower and an even longer time explaining his dirty clothes to Aunt Sara, Nick turned in for the night. He sprawled on top of his covers and let his thoughts wander. Chicago seemed far away, another lifetime. During the past two weeks, he had helped his mom sell most of their belongings, moved her in to the grandparent's apartment, and now he was a farm-hand living in the Ozarks. It seemed so long ago. In only four days, he'd turn eighteen and be showing Elmer. Could he win the prize money? Dare he dream again? He glanced over at his dad's watch and dared to hope that there would be a place in time where he would be able to fulfill his dreams.

The rooster crowed at first light, but Nick was already awake. Quickly, he threw back the covers, pulled on fresh jeans, and a green T-shirt, then raced down the hall, beating Uncle Joe to the breakfast table.

"My, you're early today." Aunt Sara scooped three pancakes from the fry pan and set them on his plate. Nick gobbled them down and asked for more. He was ready to milk cows when his uncle rose from the table.

All during milking, thoughts of the 5,000-dollar prize money filled his head. "Think I can find a good used car for 5,000 dollars, Uncle Joe?"

"A truck would make more sense around here." Uncle Joe pointed to the cow Nick was taking the milkers off of. "That left quarter isn't milked properly, Nick. Better put the milker back on her."

Nick eyed the swollen quarter seeing his mistake and did as he was told. "If I spent only 4,000 dollars on a truck maybe I would have enough money left over to take one or two courses at that university Aunt Sara was talking about." Nick hurried from cow to cow in his haste to get done, so he could work with Elmer.

"You're a good worker, Nick, and I've got an offer for you. If you win on Saturday, how about taking the money and buying five milk cows? The farm down the road has some springing heifers for sale. Those five cows would make you a steady income."

"But, I need wheels Uncle Joe, not some old cows." Nick wasn't very enthused about milking and working with animals the rest of his life.

"Let met show you something." After the cows were milked and the parlor cleaned, Uncle Joe and Nick walked up to an old shed which stood along side the workshop. Uncle Joe shoved the overhead door up, causing it to squeal on its rusty tracks. Sunlight fell on an old, yellow, Chevy truck.

"What's this?" Nick looked at the nearest fender, which was held on with duck tape. It was missing a rear bumper and tailgate.

"This here's Bobbie's truck. He bought it at a government auction. It was an old park ranger truck at one time. Bobbie put in a new engine, now it runs like a champ. It will even pull the stock trailer. This hitch is welded right to the frame." Uncle Joe pointed to a shiny steel ball mounted on the rear end.

"Why are you showing me this?" Nick questioned. He wasn't really impressed with the beat-up set of wheels.

"Invest your 5,000 dollars into the cows and you can drive Bobbie's truck back and forth to the university." Uncle Joe touched the hood, his eyes were getting misty.

Nick was speechless. He didn't want to offend his uncle, but he had pictured himself behind the wheel of a black 4X4 Dodge Ram, not a yellow *park ranger truck*. Nick glanced over at his uncle and noticed the faraway look in his eyes. He knew he would have to be careful of what he said next. "Thanks for your offer. That's really kind. Mmm... I'll think on it for a bit, okay?"

Uncle Joe rubbed the dented metal fondly. "Want to take her for a spin?"

"Well, Ahh... I've got to work Elmer. Maybe, later." Nick made a hasty retreat to the hay barn.

Just like yesterday, Rob was perched on the top board of Elmer's pen, chewing on a piece of hay. He was dressed in the same ragged clothes as yesterday and looked just as pale. "I already fed him for ya, *Yank*. I even brushed some of the dust off. Hop in here and let's see what we can do with this hunk of beef." Rob dropped down off the board and into Elmer's pen.

Nick grabbed the halter and lead rope and crawled between the boards. After fitting the halter around his face and ears, Nick and Rob took turns leading Elmer around the pen. Elmer loved the attention and gave them no problems. Gaining confidence, Nick felt it was time to lead Elmer out of his pen.

"Let's take him over to the well-house where there is a hose and give him a bath." Nick was excited about sprucing Elmer up. Rob swung the gate open and Nick led him through. He walked Elmer down the aisle of the hay barn and out the double doors. Elmer followed like a gentleman. There wasn't any place to tie Elmer by the well-house, so Rob volunteered to hold the rope while Nick did the washing.

Nick borrowed some dish soap from Aunt Sara, and he found an old brush and sponge in a bucket in the workshop. Elmer seemed to enjoy his bath and patiently stood still until Nick began brushing off the extra water. Elmer began backing up, trying to get away from the brush's stiff bristles, and Rob was having trouble stopping him.

"Grab hold, Nick, he's getting away from me." The heels of Rob's black boots were digging into the gravel, leaving a twin set of marks, but Elmer was still gaining speed. Finally, Rob had to let the rope go, as it was burning his hands. Elmer kicked up his heels, happy to be free, and galloped off down the drive towards the gravel road.

Nick threw the brush down in disgust and watched Elmer disappear from sight. "That's just great. There goes my prize-winning bull. This stuff always happens to me."

"Don't just stand there feeling sorry for yourself, *Yank*, go after him. That's a lot of steaks and pot roasts getting away." Rob said, as he rubbed his sore hands together.

Nick ran down the drive in hot pursuit of Elmer. When he reached the gravel road he stopped, looked in both directions, but didn't see any trace of the bull. He looked closely at the gravel and spotted a faint set of prints leading down Friendship Drive to the right. He began to jog down the road keeping his eyes pealed on the prints. He hadn't gone far when he saw Elmer. He was standing by the side of the road with his head nestled deep in a pile of green grass. But he wasn't alone. A young girl loosely held his lead rope in one hand, while the other held the reins of a black appaloosa.

CHAPTER SIX

EY, THERE! DOES this Bull belong to you by chance?" Nick walked up to the girl's side and she handed him the lead rope. "Hi! I'm Amy Hines." Amy patted the neck of her horse. "This is Princess." Princess nodded her head as if saying hello, flicked a fly off her hind quarters with a long black tail, and impatiently stamped a front foot.

"You just saved my life." Nick bent over at the waist trying to catch his breath. "How did you catch Elmer?"

"He just stopped when he saw me coming. I saw the lead rope trailing behind him, so I knew he belonged to someone. I just hopped off Princess and grabbed up his rope. He seems to be enjoying the fresh grass. You live close by?"

"Yeah." Nick straightened up and stretched his back out. "I'm Nick Hill. I'm staying with my aunt and uncle on Sunny Hill Dairy. I'm helping my Uncle Joe milk cows."

"You have a northern accent, where'd you come from?"

"Chicago."

"No kidding. My dad and I moved here in June, from Northbrook. That's about a forty-five minute drive west from Chicago. Ever heard of it?"

"Yeah. I've heard of it." Nick yanked Elmer's head out of the grass and began leading him down the road towards home. Amy walked beside him leading Princess.

"You staying with your uncle long or are you going back when school starts?"

"I'm out of school, graduated in May." Elmer was trying to pull Nick back over to the side of the road where some nice, tasty grass grew. "I plan on staying for awhile, I guess." Nick was fighting him for control.

"Bet you miss your mom and dad. I know I missed my mom and brother at first when we moved down here, but things are better for me now. I talk with my mom once a week and my dad tries real hard to be there for me. He even started his own business just so he'd be home more. Of course, I organize his schedule and help out with the accounting. I try to help with the housework and cook our meals, but I have rather limited cooking skills. So we have carry-out a lot." Amy shut-up and looked down at the gravel road realizing her mouth was running away.

"My dad died two months ago. I never did much with him, like camping or playing ball, but it seems that now he's gone, everywhere I look I see dead people. Sometimes, I really think I'm losing it." Nick didn't mean to confess all that to a complete stranger, but he felt better for getting it off his chest.

"It must be weird having your dad die. I lost my mom in a divorce, but I can still call and talk to her when I want. Your dad is gone for good." Amy sure could sympathize with Nick.

When they had reached the driveway, Elmer began picking up speed. He jerked the lead rope from Nick's hand and trotted up to the hay barn.

"Come on. I have to get him back in his pen." Nick took off in a run worried about capturing the mischievous bull. However, he had nothing to worry about as Elmer was standing in his pen pulling hay from the manger. Nick unsnapped the lead rope and slid the halter over his massive head. "You're a handful, Bud." After hanging up the halter and lead, he checked to make sure Elmer had plenty of fresh water. He secured the heavy gate on the pen and then he walked out of the hay barn. He saw Amy talking to Uncle Joe by the well-house. Rob was nowhere in sight. Princess was tied to a near-by fence-post. She had her eyes closed and one hind leg was propped up on the tip of her hoof. Her bottom lip drooped as she snoozed.

As Nick approached, Uncle Joe turned away and walked into the shed where the yellow truck sat. He opened the front door and started the engine. It fired on the first try. "Come on kids. Take her round the block."

Nick dropped his head and whispered into Amy's ear. "You don't have to go if you don't want to, I'll understand."

"No, that's okay, it will be fun. Let's drive over to my place. You can meet my dad. It's just down the road." Amy walked over to the passenger door and hopped inside.

Reluctantly, Nick squeezed behind the wheel. He noticed a brown leather pouch sitting on the seat between them and pointed at it. "That yours?"

"Nope. You ever drive this truck before?"

"Never. Glad it's automatic and not a shift." Nick backed the truck out of the shed being careful not to spook the horse, or worse, run over his uncle. He made a three point turn, then drove the truck down the drive. He turned right on Friendship Drive, as per Amy's instructions.

As Nick drove, Amy picked up the leather pouch and looked inside. "It's empty. Nothing but a bit of old crumbs." She tossed it down, back on the seat between them. "Turn here, this is where I live. Pull up to the garage, Dad's working out there."

Nick drove the heavy truck with ease. It really handled nicely. Maybe he would ask his uncle if he could borrow it to haul Elmer to the show on Saturday. After he won first place he'd return the truck to his uncle and buy himself some decent wheels. Nick pulled up to the garage, put the truck in park, and turned off the engine.

While wiping his hands on a rag, Mr. Hines walked up to the passenger door, and was surprised to find Amy inside. "Where's Princess? You hurt?"

"Everything's cool, Dad. I want you to meet Nick Hill. He's staying up the road on his uncle's dairy. I helped him rescue his bull today."

"Hi, Nick." Alan stuck his hand inside the open window and the men shook hands.

"Pleased to meet you, Mr. Hines. You've got a great place here."

"Call me Alan. Were did you get that haversack?" Alan pointed to the worn leather pouch.

"Haversack? It was in the truck." Amy passed the bag across Nick and out the window to her dad who began to inspect it. "See this C stamped onto the flap. It's probably from the Civil War, Calvary." Nick was glad he hadn't touched the bag after all.

Surprised, Amy asked, "How come you know so much about that?" Amy took back the pouch and traced the raised C with her index finger. She knew her dad didn't know much about history.

"Tomorrow we're going on a field trip to Wilson Creek and Crystal Cave. They are both located in Springfield, Missouri. I was reading a brochure about Sweeny's War Museum thinking we may stop there, too. They collect all kinds of stuff like that. They showed pictures of some of the stuff they collect on the cover of their brochure. A pouch just like that was shown. Didn't think your dad was so smart, did ya?" Alan rocked back on his heels proud of his knowledge.

While Alan was talking, Nick was thinking about the pocketknife he had tossed into the slime covered pond and the canteen, hanging on a tree branch, back in the woods. He wasn't going to touch either of those again either.

"Want to go with us tomorrow, Nick?   You're welcome to come along." Alan invited.

"Please come." Amy waited for his answer.

Nick wasn't really listening and didn't know where they were going, but the thought of getting off the farm for a day sounded enticing. "Sure. Just so I'm home before chores at 5. I'm helping my uncle with the milking and he would be mad if I weren't back in time."

"We'll pick you up at 8 AM. That work for you?" Alan walked over to Amy's open window and bent over beside the truck. He picked up a tiny black and gray puppy that had wandered off the porch. "Rocky misses you." He held the dog close to Amy's face. A pink tongue darted out and licked her nose before she could fend him off.

Amy giggled. "I'll ride Princess home soon, Dad." She used the palm of her hand to wipe her nose clean of Rocky's spit.

"We'll see ya later. I'll be looking forward to the trip tomorrow. Thanks for the invite." Nick started up the truck and drove back to Sunny Hill Dairy. Carefully, he parked the old truck back in the shed.

Princess was patiently waiting exactly where they had left her. Amy stepped out of the truck, turned, and waved goodbye. "See ya tomorrow, Nick. We'll have fun in the cave; my vote is still out on the battlefield thing."

Nick waved back, but continued sitting in the truck. In the rear-view mirror, he watched Amy swing up on Princess's back and trot off down the drive. When she was out of sight he looked at the haversack sitting next to him on the seat. He knew he shouldn't touch it, but his curiosity got the best of him. Slowly, he rested the palm of his right hand on the raised C. He was ready as his world changed. He saw a young boy sitting on his heels close to a small fire. His face looked older than his years. His hands were cupped around a tin mug, and he was chewing a strip of beef jerky. A silver sword was in a scabbard fastened securely to his side. A strawberry-roan stood saddled nearby.

CHAPTER SEVEN

s Nick watched the scene, four riders cantered into the young boy's camp. As the men talked to the boy, he quickly kicked dirt over the hot embers of his fire, drank down the liquid in the tin cup, and tucked it into the haversack slung over his shoulder. Gathering together his horse's reins, he swung up onto the mare's back, and sat firmly in the saddle. He pulled the silver sword from its case, pointed it forward, and cantered off with the other riders, who looked like they were charging after the enemy.

Nick removed his hand from the raised C and the vision faded from sight. Nick was once again back on his uncle's farm, sitting in a yellow park ranger truck, in a dark shed. For a moment he almost wished that he too could ride off with that boy. Somehow he would love to avenge his father's untimely death.

In the distance, Nick heard his aunt calling, "Lunch is ready. Come and get it."

Nick grabbed the haversack and stuffed it into the space behind the seat. He saw a dirty pair of yellow gloves stashed under the seat. He spread them over the top of the bag, effectively hiding it from sight. He got out of the truck and hurried inside the house to clean himself up for another delicious meal.

As he ate the last bite of his peach cobbler, his aunt set a cardboard box next to his place. "This came in the mail for you today. It looks like it's from your mom. I bet she sent you a gift for your birthday on Saturday. Want to wait or open it now?"

The return address was his grandparent's apartment in Chicago. Nick looked at his aunt and smiled, then quickly tore open the box. Inside, carefully surrounded by Styrofoam peanuts, was a digital camera, a black leather carrying case, and a black neck strap. Putting the camera off to the side, he opened the attached card and read:

> Happy Birthday Son! 18 years today. Thought you would enjoy taking pictures of your new place. Please send me some photos so I can picture you there. Your grandparents are driving me batty. I am going to find a job next week just to get out of here for a bit. Glad you choose the farm. I plan to take the bus down over Christmas for a visit. Looking forward to seeing you,
>
> Love Mom

Nick passed around the camera and note for everyone to read. After they all had a chance to examine the new goods, Uncle Joe said, "Mr. Peebles, from MilkyWay Dairy, came over while you were test driving the truck. He's willing to sell you five heifers in case you're interested. I told him you'd let him know after the show on Saturday."

Inwardly Nick groaned. He didn't want to buy any smelly cows. "Thanks for asking, it's always good to know, right?" Quickly changing the subject Nick asked, "By the way, can I use the yellow truck to haul Elmer to the show on Saturday?"

"You bet. She's all yours. Bobbie used to call her his, *Little Honey Bee.*" Uncle Joe pushed himself away from the table and stretched out on the living room sofa for a bit of shut-eye.

"Thanks for lunch, Aunt Sara." Nick grabbed his new camera, inserted the enclosed batteries, and snapped a picture of his aunt clearing the table.

"Oh, Nicky! My hair looks awful" She tried tucking the stray hair around her face back into her barrette.

"You looked just fine. I'm going to take a few pictures outside." Nick clicked off several shots of the house, the yard, and the barns. He walked into the hay barn and snapped one of Rose. He saw Rob sitting, as usual, on the top board of Elmer's pen. "Can I take your photo, Rob?"

"Click away, *Yank.* Where'd you get the fancy camera?"

"It's a birthday gift from my mom." Nick shot two pictures of Rob, then turned and aimed the lens at Elmer, and shot a few more.

"Birthday you say, well I've got a gift for ya, but I didn't bring it today." Rob shifted the piece of hay he was chewing to the other side of his mouth. "Hey, **Yank**, did you happen to see a leather pouch around here? I had my lunch packed in it and now I can't find the blasted thing."

"I found a brown haversack on the truck seat earlier, but it was empty."

"That be it. Where's it now?" Rob jumped off the board and hurried towards the door.

Nicked yelled after his retreating form, "Look behind the truck seat, under some yellow gloves. But I tell ya, it's empty, there's no lunch inside." Nick watched Rob until he was out of sight. Quickly he snuck a peak at the pictures he had just shot. Perfect! There was a great shot of Rob. Now he could show Uncle Joe and finally find out who this strange boy was.

As Nick waited for Rob to return, he tossed another flake of hay into Elmer's manger. As he worked, he remembered watching Amy stick her hand inside the bag. She had found nothing but crumbs inside. Done with his task, Nick sat down on a nearby hay bale and fiddled some more with his camera.

Rob came back into the barn carrying the haversack that was in the truck. He sat down crossed legged on the dirt floor resting his back against the rough boards of Elmer's pen. He opened the flap of the bag and pulled out a tin cup. It was stuffed full of some kind of shrivel up meat. Nick's jaw fell open, as he watched Rob place it on the floor beside him. Rob's hand dove back into the pouch and pulled out a silver frame with a black and white picture inside it. He handed the picture over to Nick.

"That's me. What you're looking at is a new photographic process called an *ambrotype*. Ever heard of that? Better than your camera, right, **Yank**? Now that's a pretty good image of me, if I don't say so myself. Had it taken for dear old, Mom."

Nick stared at the fuzzy face in the photo that had turned yellow with age. When he looked up he saw that Rob was chewing on a piece of the dried meat.

"Hey, what ya staring at? You want a bite of this? It's beef jerky, real tasty." Rob extended what looked like a piece of shoe leather towards him.

"No, thanks, just had dinner." Nick handed the picture back. "Where'd you say you had this picture taken?"

"Didn't say, **Yank**. Asking trick questions, ain't ya? You'd make a good spy." Rob fumbled around in the sack and pulled out a white cracker. He broke off a piece and stuffed it in his mouth and chewed noisily.

Nick was sure that sack had been empty when he had held it last. Nick thought back to when he touched the raised C. He tried to focus on what he thought he had seen. He thought he remembered seeing a young boy sitting before a fire, holding a tin cup and eating jerky. He quickly snapped off another shot of Rob, surrounded by the articles taken out of the pouch.

Nick was curious about the white cracker. "That looks awful hard to chew, what is it?"

"This? It's hardtack, *Yank*. Hardtack. I can almost live off this stuff. It can get wormy, so ya have to guard against moisture. It's a favorite food of the Confederate Army, don't cha know."

CHAPTER EIGHT

UST AS NICK was going to question Rob about the hardtack and his comment about the Civil War, he heard his uncle walk into the barn. "You in there, Nicky boy?"

"I'm back by Elmer." Nick stood and faced his uncle. Glad you're here. I'd like you to meet Rob McFarley."

"Who? Don't see anyone 'cept Elmer and I already know him." Uncle Joe laughed at his own joke.

Nick turned around and looked to where Rob had been sitting, but found the spot empty. No tin cup, no beef jerky, no hardtack, no Rob. "How could he disappear so fast?" Nick looked into the dark corners of the barn.

"I'll meet him some other time. Come on kid, we've got to get chores started."

Nick walked beside his uncle down to the milk house. Together they began the evening chores. Nick took a few pictures of Uncle Joe milking the cows.

As they worked Nick asked, "Would it be okay if I go to Springfield to-morrow with the Hines? They invited me along. They are going to visit a cave and a battlefield or something. I could use a break from this farm." Nick wished he hadn't added the last part. His uncle was frowning and it didn't look encouraging.

"What about Elmer? Don't you need to work with him? You only have three days left to get him ready to show. You know you will have to put in more work, if you plan on winning first place. The competition will be brutal." It was clear that his uncle wasn't really happy about his missing a day working with Elmer.

""Elmer is coming along nicely, well, as long as he's enclosed in a pen. I'll be home for chores, and I'll work with him afterwards." Nick slipped his camera into his pocket. "Is there a place where I can get these picture printed? I want to send my mom some shots of your farm." In truth, what Nick really wanted was to print out the pictures of Rob and all the stuff that was in the haversack.

"Wal-mart prints photos. That's where your aunt and I always take ours. Yeah, go have fun tomorrow." With both men working, the chores were done quickly. Nick bottle fed Rose and checked on Elmer making sure he was all set for the night. Rob was nowhere in sight.

After Nick and Uncle Joe showered, Aunt Sara served everyone a bowl of vanilla ice cream with hot chocolate sauce dribbled over the top. Nick took his bowl outside and ate under the stars. While the cool treat slipped down his throat, he silently formed questions in his mind to ask Alan tomorrow. A two-hour drive would give him plenty of time to learn some valuable information about running an electronic business. Maybe, someday, Nick would have his own business, maybe... Nick stopped himself from going down that road. He'd just better concentrate on winning Saturday. He needed to focus on one step at a time; making just one piece of his dream come true, just one.

Nick was up before the rooster crowed on Thursday morning. He wanted to surprise his uncle by bringing the cows in to be milked without his help. He refused his aunt's big breakfast, instead grabbing a couple pieces of toast. He was out the door before his uncle sat down to eat.

Nick hurried through chores, showered and dressed in clean shorts, a dark blue T-shirt and sandals, by 8 AM. The Hines picked him up in their Ford Escort right on time. He grabbed his camera, said his goodbyes, and slipped into the backseat.

"Ready for a road trip?" Amy looked over her shoulder at Nick and flashed him a smile.

"You bet I'm ready." Nick noticed the unusual necklace around her neck. A golden brown stone hung on a leather strap. "What kind of stone is that?"

"It's amber. A friend of mine gave it to me for my birthday. It's very special to me." Amy rubbed the stone between her fingers.

Her answer reminded Nick about his friend, Rob and the pictures he wanted to print off. "Can we stop off at a Wal-mart if it's on the way? I'd like to print off some pictures."

"The Wal-mart in Mountain Grove has a printing service. Let's stop on the way home. How's that sound?" Alan was busy adjusting the knobs on the air conditioner. Dark stains were forming on the back of his shirt, and under his arms. "Boy, it's hot today."

"Yeah. That works. How did you become interested in electronics? I'm interested in computers." Nick placed his camera on the seat and sat forward to hear Alan's answer.

"I took a course at Northwestern University in Chicago back in the '70's. From there..." Alan and Nick talked shop for the whole drive. Amy was glad to see the Springfield exit and pointed out the sign to Wilson Creek. "Here's our exit, Dad. Don't miss it."

Wilson Creek was ten miles south of the city. The battlefield was a national park. Alan parked the car outside the information center. The three of them went inside and listened to an informative narration of the battles. They learned that over 12,000 soldiers fighting for the Confederates under General Price, clashed with 6,000 Union soldiers led by General Lyon.

For five hours on the morning of August 10th, 1861, the battle raged on the crest of a ridge, later named Bloody Hill for the slaughter that occurred there. By 11 AM the Union forces had exhausted their ammunition supply, forcing them to retreat. They left behind, to remain forever, 1,317 Union soldiers and 1,222 Confederates.

Alan bought a pass to tour the battlefield from the car. It was a 4.9 mile, one-way loop, passing all the historic points of the battle. He followed the paved road through dense woods, passing over Wilson Creek and arriving at a clearing that was once Gibbon's oat field. They passed Ray's cornfield, which fed the hungry Confederate soldiers. They saw the old Wire Road, a narrow dirt path leading up to the battlefield. It was used to transport the heavy artillery. Finally, they arrived at Bloody Hill. They parked in a small lot and walked up the trail to the famous ridge. An old cannon sat with its mouth pointed in the direction to repel the Union attack. A stack of cannon balls sat nearby. Nick looked over the battlefield, now overgrown with weeds and brush. He could picture the battle in his mind. He remembered the vision he had of the soldier who was slumped against some boulders, shot in the chest, dying, with his horse and silver sword by his side.

The air was still; no breeze stirred these hallowed grounds. His ears could almost hear the long ago rifle shots and cannon thunder. He felt the ghosts of the fallen, deep within his soul.

A plaque honoring the brave soldiers who fought and died on these grounds stood off to the side. Blue coats fighting Gray, each believing their way was right. Nick read down the list of strangers. His eyes froze when he saw a familiar name: Rob McFarley- Died August 10, 1861.

Suddenly, Nick felt like he'd been suckered punched in the gut. He just couldn't catch his breath. His forehead broke out in a sweat and his legs felt shaky.

CHAPTER NINE

EY, NICK. ARE you okay? Here, sit down a minute. You look pale." Alan guided Nick by the elbow over to a stone bench, placed under the shade of an oak tree. "Put your head between your knees. You'll be fine in a second. It's this heat and no breeze." Alan pushed Nick's head down.

After a few minutes, Nick sat back up, finally able to take a deep breath. "I'm better. Can we go? I just want to go." Nick stood, stumbled a few steps and began to walk up the path towards where the car was parked.

"What's wrong with him?" Amy came up behind her dad giving him a quick hug. "He looks like he saw a ghost." They both followed Nick down the path and back to the car. Alan unlocked the Escort and they piled in. Alan checked Nick out in the rear-view mirror. He was staring out the window, deep in thought, and taking a lot of deep breaths. His color was back, thank goodness. Alan sure didn't know how to treat any illnesses.

"Enough battlefields. How about some fun in a cool cave? Heard they stay about sixty- degrees all year round." Alan tried to be a competent tour guide, but he got no response from Nick. He looked at Amy and shrugged his shoulders. Starting the car, he drove his little tour group away from Wilson Creek. He drove about six miles north of Springfield to Crystal Cave.

The further they drove away from Bloody Hill, the better Nick began to feel. The tightness in his chest began to fade, making it easier for him to breath. Being on the battlefield, surrounded by all that death, had knocked the wind from him. Seeing Rob McFarley's name on the plaque was a shock. What were the chances of a soldier, who was killed over 100 years ago, of having the same name as his friend, Rob? Rob McFarley, his new friend back in Raymondville, who sat on a board by Elmer's pen, chewing a piece of hay. Nick's mind was swirling, trying to make sense of the connection. Was Rob dead? How could that be? Impossible.

Nick pictured the last time he had seen his dad. His face was cold and shiny, like a piece of marble. His eyes were closed; his hands were crossed over his chest, as he lay, so still, in a coffin lined with white satin. He remembered carrying the coffin out of the church to the waiting hearse. Now his dad was buried under the earth, no different than the soldiers who died in battle.

Then his mind flashed back to his friend, Rob McFarley, in worn clothes, sunken eyes and bony hands. Who was he? Why didn't his uncle know him? He knew everyone in the neighborhood. Nothing made sense. By the time they pulled into the Crystal Cave parking lot, Nick had gotten his emotions back under control and he was breathing normal again. The thoughts of death were fading.

Alan parked the car and said, "Everyone stick close together. I've heard there are man-eating bats down there." Alan joked around trying to lighten Nick's dark mood. "I'll go purchase the tickets and see what time the next tour is." Alan got out of the car and walked towards the door of the cave's souvenir shop.

Amy turned around in her seat and looked at Nick. "What happened back there? You looked like you saw a ghost."

"I saw my friend's name on the grave marker. I think that he was the solider killed in battle."

"How can your friend be killed in a war over 100 years ago? You're not making any sense Nick. Maybe he's a cousin or something; lots of people have the same names."

"I know that now, but I just felt something weird back at the battlefield. I felt I knew that soldier and I felt his fear just before he was shot. Then, I began to remember my dad and the pain I felt when I learned he was killed. Everything just all ran together." Nick shook his head and wiped his hair back from his forehead. "Don't worry, I'm better now."

"You must care a lot for your new friend."

"He's helping me with Elmer. In his own way, he's not letting me forget my dreams."

Glancing out the window, Amy saw her dad waving at them. "Look. There's Dad. Let's go." Amy and Nick climbed from the car, locked the doors and met Alan by the side of the cave building.

"We're in luck. The tour is about to start. It's just us and that guy over there with the two kids." Alan pointed to a man with three cameras slung around his neck. "You got your camera, Nick?"

"Yeah." Nick unwound the strap and put it around his neck, so his hands would be free for exploring the cave.

Their guide appeared by the trail leading into the cave. He was wearing a pair of denim overalls and muddy work boots. He walked with stooped shoulders and had a long gray ponytail hanging out from under a faded blue baseball hat with, *OUTDOOR WORLD,* across the front. "Follow me." He wasn't one to waste words.

The old man turned and began walking down a dirt path leading into the woods. After a short walk, the path descended into a deep hole. Their way was lit by light bulbs every twenty feet. "Watch your step and your head. The ceilings are low in spots. We are going down into the earth, over 100 feet."

Using a handrail for balance, the group descended. They immediately noticed the change in temperature- from eighty-five degrees to a cool sixty. The cave was damp and dark. Everyone stood in a circle, as they listened to the guide talking in almost a whisper.

"The Indians first found this cave back in the mid 1800's. They climbed down this sinkhole to escape the nasty winters. Outside, it can be zero degrees, but in here it's always sixty. Behind you is a stream which they used for drinking and cooking." He shined his flashlight onto the roof of the cave. "There you can see the soot from their fires. And right there is a brown bat hanging by his feet. They are frequent visitors to our cave. Please do not attempt to touch them." He shined the light over to the floor by the back wall. "Right there an important Indian chief was buried; his bones lay undisturbed. Stay close together and follow me."

"Watch for ghosts, Nick." Amy poked him in the ribs with her elbow.

The guide showed them many natural wonders of the cave, Nick flashing his camera at the most unusual. The guide pointed out a formation that resembled a Washington monument. One room looked like a cathedral, all the rock looking like lace. He pointed to soda straw stalactites hanging from the ceiling, which are still active to this day. They spent two hours climbing through tunnels on their hands and knees, stooping through narrow passages, and squeezing sideways between rock walls. Nick enjoyed the beauty of the cave and their guide's informative narration, but he was glad to see daylight, and feel the summer's heat once again.

"Thanks for taking me here, Alan. I enjoyed the tour." Nick climbed into the back seat of the Escort, placing his camera on the seat next to him.

"Sorry, you didn't enjoy Wilson Creek. Amy told me about your dad and maybe it wasn't a good idea that we went there." Alan started the car turning the air conditioner on full blast.

"No. It wasn't about my dad. Well, maybe a bit, but couldn't you feel what must have happened there?"

"It was hot. I do admit to that. Now, how about some lunch? Lone Star for a steak and potato?" Alan drove out of the cave parking lot and back towards Springfield for a tasty lunch.

"Maybe Nick would prefer beef jerky and hardtack." Amy teased. Nick yanked her ponytail in response.

After a tummy stretching meal of: rib eye, baked potato smothered in cheese, sour cream and butter, bread and salad, Alan drove the little group east to the Mountain Grove Wal-mart. He stayed in the car to grab a short nap, while Nick and Amy ran in and printed off the pictures he had taken earlier. Back in the car, Nick ripped opened the package of printed pictures. As they traveled back to Raymondville, where the cows were waiting to be milked, Nick studied the pictures.

"Let's see!" Amy stuck her hand over the seat reaching for the stack of pictures.

"Hang on a sec..." Nick raced through the shots of the house, the cows and the barns, looking for the two he took of Rob McFarley. There they were! The boards of Elmer's pen with the bull's head showing in the background came out great. But there was no image of Rob perched on the top board. He just wasn't there. Nick quickly thumbed to the photo he took of Rob eating his lunch on the dirt floor. He especially wanted to see the haversack, the tin cup, the picture frame, the beef jerky, and the hardtack. He needed to see proof that these things existed. But the picture was dark, filled with shadows. He couldn't see any of the shapes clearly.

CHAPTER TEN

ICK KEPT STARING at the two pictures in his hand. "Drats. I thought for sure I had him this time."

"Had who?" Amy's hand held the rest of the pictures, except the two Nick was staring at.

"I'm talking about Rob. I had pointed the camera right at him, twice. I even saw him on the camera screen after taking the picture. However, when I printed out the pictures of him, he doesn't appear in the photo."

"Well, I can explain that. Sometimes when you think you're taking someone's picture your thumb's over the lens. I do that all the time. That's probably what happened." Amy handed him back the stack of printed pictures.

"No. I'm sure I took his picture." Nick scratched the side of his head in frustration.

Listening to the conversation, Alan was beginning to think that Nick's train wasn't following a straight track into the station. He'd make a great computer geek, they all marched to a different drummer. "Looks like we'll have you back for chore time." Alan pulled into the drive of Sunny Hill Dairy right at five, and pointed out across the field. "I see that your uncle is bringing in the cows."

"Thanks for the great day guys." Nick climbed out of the car. "I really had a good time."

Amy wasn't ready to say goodbye yet. "You want to go for a horse ride some day?" She couldn't tear her eyes away from him.

"Sure, that sounds like fun." Nick began walking away, but then turned back to the car. "Hey, I'm going to be showing Elmer at the livestock show on Saturday in Houston. Would you like to go?" Nick hadn't planned on asking her. Normally he was a loner and never looked twice at girls. "Rob will be along with me, so there won't be much room in the truck, but if you want to go we'll squeeze you in."

"Great. About what time?" Amy's eyes lit up with joy at being asked. She would be trying on every pair of jeans she owned for the next two days deciding what looked best.

"Let's see.... The show begins at noon. I'll pick you up at 10:00. That should give us enough time to get checked in and get Elmer ready. Thanks again for everything, Alan." Nick waved bye and walked to the house to change into his barn clothes. By the time Nick arrived in the milk house, his uncle was milking the first group of cows.

"Have a good day in Springfield?" Uncle Joe asked as he attached a milker to a swollen udder.

Nick shrugged his shoulder. "It was okay. Alan drove us around the Wilson Creek Battlefield and then we took a tour of Crystal Cave. That was cool. He bought us lunch at Lone Star." Nick began preparing the other cows for milking. He didn't have to ask what to do anymore; he had the routine down pat.

"Get your pictures printed?"

"Yeah. They turned out fine. I'll write Mom tomorrow and send her some."

"You won't have time tomorrow. I've got some plans of my own. I'm taking you to town to buy you your birthday present. Elmer needs a shiny new halter and you need some fancy show clothes, maybe even a hat. I thought that would make the perfect birthday gift for you. When we are done shopping, I'm taking you to Cabool, so you can check out the courses Drury University has to offer. We'll even check into the available scholarships."

"Do you think I've got a chance for one?"

"You won't know unless you try. You're a smart kid and you had good grades in high school. Give it your best shot if it's important to you."

"Thanks, Uncle Joe. I really appreciate your help."

Uncle Joe and Nick milked side-by-side, working the groups of cows until they were down to the last four. "I'll finish up here. You go work with Elmer. Don't forget to feed Rose."

Nick grabbed Rose's bottle of milk and walked to the hay barn. On the way he thought about college. If he worked hard he could afford to take one course this fall. Or if he won the $5,000 prize money he could... Rose eagerly drank down her milk, mooing for more. Nick scratched behind her ears and watched her butt the bars of the pen searching for more milk.

A voice over by Elmer's pen startled him. "Where ya been, *Yank?* We've got to work Elmer. Can't expect to win, if you don't have your bull in shape."

Nick tossed the bottle on the ground and walked back to Elmer's pen. "Sorry, Rob. I went to Springfield today with Amy and Alan, our neighbors. I printed those photos I took of you yesterday." Nick dug into the rear pocket of his jeans and pulled out the two pictures he had stashed there. He handed them up to Rob, who was sitting on the top board of the pen, as usual.

"Nice color shot of Elmer's head. What's this? A picture of the floor? Bad subject matter, *Yank.*"

"I took them of you, Rob, but you're not in them."

Rob was flipping between the two photos when his fingers slipped and they fluttered into Elmer's pen landing on the manure pack. "Oops. My bad." Rob leaped down off the boards, bent over, and reached for the pictures.

Elmer saw Rob's exposed butt as a perfect target and couldn't resist the temptation. He tucked his head and charged.

"Rob! Watch out!" Nick saw what was about to happen, but was helpless to prevent it. BAM! Elmer hit Rob hard, and sent him flying head first into the boards. Rob hit with a sickening thud. Nick quickly opened the gate and slipped into the pen, careful to secure it behind him. "Back. Move back." He waved his hands in front of Elmer to distract him. Elmer's target was gone; his game was over. He obeyed Nick and stepped backward, away from the crumpled form.

Nick knelt by Rob's side, while keeping one eye on the bull. "Rob. Rob. Can you hear me?"

"Water. I need water." Rob whispered a raspy plea.

"Don't move. I'll get water and Uncle Joe. He'll know what to do." Nick grabbed Elmer's rope and halter, tying him tightly to the boards on the opposite side of the pen. Then he raced to the house looking for his uncle.

"Uncle Joe! Uncle Joe!" Nick burst into the kitchen only to find a note tucked under the cow napkin holder on the table.

UNCLE JOE AND I WENT TO TOWN TO RENT A MOVIE. HAM SANDWICH IN FRIDGE, HELP YOURSELF. WE'LL BE BACK SOON. LOVE AUNT SARA

Nick filled a plastic glass with water and grabbed the ham sandwich. Food always made people feel better. He ran back to Elmer's pen where he saw Rob laid flat on his back, eyes closed. His face was deathly pale and his eyes looked black and sunken, more so than normal. "Rob. Rob. Please be okay."

"Hush, Yank. You're talking loud enough to wake the dead. I'm fine. I was just taking a cat-nap. Now give me the water. Hey, what else did you bring?" Rob pulled himself into a sitting position with his back leaning against the boards of the pen, his legs sticking straight out. Nick handed him the sandwich. He took a bite, washing it down with the water. "This is great! Much better than jerky."

"Nothing broke?" Can you move?" Nick hovered over Rob like a nervous hen over her eggs come hatching time.

"Relax. 'Fraid I ruined your photos." Rob pointed to the crumpled pictures covered in manure.

Nick and Rob heard the tires of the farm truck crunching on the gravel outside the hay barn door. It stopped and his aunt leaned out the window and said, "Nick. We're back. We rented the movie, Gettysburg. We thought since you were at Wilson Creek all day studying the Civil War, you'd like to watch this. It's four hours long, so hurry in." Uncle Joe drove the truck over to the workshop and parked.

"Gettysburg. Now that's a battle you *Yanks* won. You'll like that one." Rob was devouring the sandwich like there was no tomorrow.

"I'm not going to watch it. I've seen enough death for one day."

"I reckon you can stand a tad more. Here, take this." Rob held his hand out to Nick. "I got it at Wilson Creek."

"When were you at Wilson Creek?" Nick extended his hand towards Rob's hand, palm open. "What is it?"

Rob dropped a smooth piece of flattened lead onto it. "That there's a bullet, Yank. A bullet. Caught it in my chest."

CHAPTER ELEVEN

 ICK JERKED HIS hand back, but it was too late. The bullet had touched his skin. Nick swayed a bit and closed his eyes. In his mind he saw the dying soldier by the boulder, except this time the young boy of his past visions was cradling the man's head. He understood now that they were brothers. One had died on the Wilson Creek battlefield and the other had lived to carry the silver sword home to their mother, and avenge his brother's death.

Nick opened his fingers and let the bullet roll off. It dropped into the manure, lost from sight. The vision slowly faded, leaving him a bit lightheaded, but otherwise feeling okay. He opened his eyes and saw the plastic water bottle and empty sandwich bag on the ground before him. He was full of questions, but Rob was gone. Nick untied Elmer, tossed him some hay and then walked to the house.

Aunt Sara was busy working in the kitchen pouring soda into plastic glasses when Nick walked in. "Movie's ready to begin. Hurry and shower." He could smell the popcorn popping in the microwave. The buttery smell almost made him change his mind.

"I'm too tired to watch. You start without me. I'm sorry." Nick untied Bobbie's work boots and headed down the hall before his aunt could organize an argument.

He quickly showered, washing away the grime of the day, but not the thick layer of questions he still needed answers to. He put on a clean T-shirt and crawled under the covers, puling the pillow tight over his head to muffle the sounds erupting from the TV blaring from the next room. He squeezed his eyes shut, but it was a long time before his mind let him go to sleep.

The rooster crowed at dawn on Friday. Nick was already awake waiting for its call. Before crawling out from under the covers, he was picturing the cows which they were about to milk, and he realized that they weren't just cows to him anymore. He was beginning to put names to their faces and he was recognizing their different personalities. For instance, Buttercup, would only come into the parlor on the south side and only if she was first. Thelma had a stump for a tail and the sweetest disposition; never any trouble and she always stood still when you milked her.   Clopper, a dark caramel Jersey, always took her sweet time because of her long hooves. Swiss Miss, a Brown Swiss, had dark brown markings on her face, which accented her shiny black eyes, which she batted in an innocent way.

It was in that moment that Nick realized he was actually looking forward to chores. He threw off the covers, got dressed, and joined his uncle at the breakfast table. Aunt Sara had fixed a huge pan of oatmeal. Nick helped himself to a bowl, stirring in a generous amount of brown sugar and milk.

Between bites, his uncle spoke to Nick. "As soon as we finish chores this morning, we'll drive to town. Sound good to you?" Uncle Joe took a second helping-eating it straight, no milk, no sugar.

"Just so I can find time today to work with Elmer. Last night didn't go too well. I didn't really make any progress." Nick didn't want to upset his relatives by telling them about Rob's accident. It would hit too close to the heart, plus they might prevent him from taking Elmer to the competition.

"We'll take *The Little Honey Bee* and top off her gas tank, so she'll be ready for you to haul Elmer to the fair tomorrow. Then, it's off birthday shopping!" Uncle Joe was really getting into this whole birthday shopping day.

Nick used a napkin to wipe some oatmeal off his lips before answering, "Sure, that's fine with me." Nick was catching his uncle's mood and was excited about getting some fancy show clothes and some accessories for Elmer.

On the walk down to the milk house, Uncle Joe spotted Cinnamon having her baby down in the valley. He re-checked her after chores were done and discovered a newborn calf lying by her side. They would be fine until the evening chores. It looked like Nick would have another calf to feed tonight.

With Uncle Joe driving and Nick riding shotgun, they were off to town by 9:00 A.M. Their first stop was the Triple H Tack Store. Uncle Joe picked out a first class, black, leather halter with matching lead for Elmer. Nick tried on five pairs of pants before he finally settled on a black pair with silver rivets around the pockets. The owner of the store matched a belt to the pants for him. Uncle Joe picked out a flashy dark-green western shirt with an eagle embroidered across the back. Nick had never owned such a fancy shirt before. He would be proud to wear it while showing Elmer.

Nick tried on every pair of cowboy boots, in size twelve, that the owner had, but none fit quite right. Instead of boots, Uncle Joe splurged on a black cowboy hat with a silver band around it. Nick was sure to catch the judge's eye.

After stowing their new purchases in the truck, they drove down town and checked out Brown's Shoe Store and Wal-mart, but still couldn't find any boots that fit right.

"Don't worry Uncle Joe, I can polish up Bobbie's old show boots. They'll be fine for the show." Nick was so tickled with his new clothes and Elmer's show halter that he wasn't too worried about the boots. His uncle had already spent a fortune on his new gear, he didn't need to spend anymore.

The Little Honey Bee transported them to Cabool, one town south of Houston, where they stopped off at the Drury University Administration Building. Uncle Joe and Nick ventured into the registration office, apparently, no appointment was necessary. The lady behind the desk seemed to be running the whole office. She wore a colorful skirt and a bright yellow blouse. She rose to meet them.

"Welcome. I'm Martha. What can I do for you today?" She extended her hand and gave their hands a firm shake. Nick sat in a chair while Uncle Joe preferred to stand behind him.

"I want to take a course this fall. But I don't know where to start." Nick's face was turning a bright red.

"Do you have a high school diploma or a GED?" Martha questioned.

"Yeah. I have a high school diploma. I graduated in May."

"I'll need a copy of that. Here's a list of the available courses for the fall semester. What are you interested in?" Martha unfolded a pamphlet listing a choice of courses and pushed it across the desk towards Nick. "You should know that we are a satellite of the main campus, which is located in Springfield, Missouri. Our evening courses are held in the Cabool high school from 7-11 P.M. Monday thru Friday.

"That's fine. The boy's interested in computers." Uncle Joe spoke up while shifting his weight from foot to foot.

"I don't have any money. Can I qualify for any scholarships?" Nick blurted out this information rather bluntly.

"We have a school scholarship for full-time students that you will most likely qualify for. It pays forty dollars per course."

"I'll need more that that." Nick stood ready to leave. "Sorry to have wasted your time. This isn't going to work."

Martha eyed Uncle Joe's cracked and stained hands. "Are you by chance, farmers?"

Uncle Joe straightened his back. "Yes, we are. I own and operate Sunny Hill Dairy. I don't see why that should matter. Nick's a smart boy and a hard worker. Just because we are farmers..."

"Please, sit back down." Martha opened a drawer and fiddled with some papers inside. Nick sat back in the chair. "Do you work with your father on the farm, Nick?"

"He's my uncle and yes, I do." Nick was beginning to squirm under the onslaught of questions.

"I see." Martha replied, continuing with the questions. "Do you work on the farm full-time?"

"What does this have to do with scholarships?" Uncle Joe was starting to become impatient with all the questions concerning the farm.

"RMI, a Missouri based business, offers a full scholarship to students. But they only offer it to people working full-time on farms." Martha was really tickled to announce this little tidbit.

Nick's mouth dropped opened rendering him speechless. Uncle Joe had to reply for him. "A full scholarship, you say. What's the catch?"

"No catch. RMI will look over your high school grades and you must show proof of paying your nephew wages for working on the farm. Nick must attend all the necessary classes, and maintain a 3.0 grade point. An allowance for books and gas is also rewarded.

Martha helped Nick and Uncle Joe fill out the necessary forms. A copy of Nick's records would be faxed to her later today from his Chicago high school. After she studied his transcript, she would be able to give him an answer by tomorrow afternoon if he qualified for the scholarship or not.

"You take this information home and study the course selection. You will be able to enroll for fifteen credit hours, that's up to five classes. Of course, with working on the farm full-time, you should limit yourself to only four classes. Remember, you need a 3.0 grade point average. You might want to take fewer classes and do well in them, than take too many and fail. In that case, the money would be discontinued.

Nick and Uncle Joe were both so excited about this wonderful opportunity for Nick to attend college on a full scholarship, that they didn't see the black, leather boots that had been tucked between the plastic bags from the Triple H Tack Store until they were halfway home.

CHAPTER TWELVE

 ICK LOOKED OVER the truck seat at the packages stored behind it and saw a piece of black leather pecking out between the two tan bags, that they had gotten earlier from the tack store. "Hey! What's this, Uncle Joe?"

Twisting around and over the seat, Nick reached down, grabbed the leather and tugged. A tall riding boot, from between the bags, appeared. When his hand came in contact with the soft leather, his vision blurred, and he thought he saw the young soldier, whom he has seen many times before, with the silver sword strapped to his side. The soldier was on his knees proposing to a young woman. His face reflected the love he had for this slender gal and he was eagerly anticipating her answer. The soldier didn't have much to offer, no land, no home, no money, only a dream for the future.

"What is it?" Uncle Joe swerved to avoid crossing the centerline as he tried to see what Nick had pulled from between the bags.

His uncle's question had chased the vision away, but Nick still felt a warm tingle deep in his chest from the pleasant scene he had just witnessed. He liked those boots and wasn't afraid to touch them again. "Look. A pair of leather boots. Where did you find them?" Nick kicked his sandal off his foot and pushed his bare toes down the leather top, slipping firmly into the bottom. It was a perfect fit. The boots would compliment his show clothes. "Thanks, Uncle Joe. They're perfect."

"Now wait just a minute, son. I've been trying to tell ya, I didn't buy them. Heck, I've been with you the whole day. Where'd they come from?" Uncle Joe scratched the stubble growing on his chin in confusion.

Ignoring his uncle's words, Nick kept talking. "This has been the best day, *ever*. New clothes, maybe a scholarship- so I can take courses this fall, then these cool boots." He stroked the soft leather while looking out the window as they cruised over the country roads back into Houston. "Hey, Uncle Joe. Look at all those Dodge Ram's lined up in that used car lot." Nick pointed to *Speedy Motors--Used Cars of the Ozarks*. "After I win Saturday we can come here and look for trucks."

"What's wrong with *The Little Honey Bee*? She's a great truck. You're just wasting your money. What about the five heifers? They would pay for themselves plus make you money for years to come." Uncle Joe wasn't letting Nick off the hook about buying those heifers.

Nick watched the car lot until they were out of sight. He was picturing himself in the shiny black 4X4, not working on the farm. "Can we stop and buy a burger? I'm starved. I'll even treat." Nick had a few bucks left in his wallet that his mom had slipped into his pocket, before he boarded the train in Chicago. That seemed like years ago.

Uncle Joe pulled into Sonic, *"The World's Best Drive-in"*, and ordered them both cheeseburgers, fries, and chocolate shakes. The perfect American meal. With the food wrapped in paper sacks beside them, Uncle Joe drove the truck downtown, to the Emmett Kelly Clown Park, where they found a vacant table under some shade trees. The greasy smell was driving them both crazy and they couldn't wait to take their first bites.

After settling down at a table, Nick asked, "Who's Emmett Kelly?" He squeezed a plastic packet of ketchup over his fries and then sprinkled some salt on them.

"He's a world-famous clown. Houston's his home. Every year in April, many of the town people dress like clowns and march in a parade. They have awards for the best costumes. There's a carnival and lots of food to eat, all to honor his worldwide fame. Sometimes, Emmett Jr. appears in person and the crowd goes crazy." Uncle Joe sipped on his shake, then took a bite of his burger. "Mmm… this sure is good."

Uncle Joe and Nick enjoyed the company of each other. They were both careful to avoid talk about purchasing the five heifers, buying a new truck, or where the mysterious boots came from.

After lunch was consumed, they disposed of their trash and climbed back into the yellow park ranger truck. "I've one more stop to make, then we can go home and you can try Elmer's new halter on him."

Uncle Joe parked in front of Forbes Drug Store. Nick tagged along behind his uncle, looking at the variety of goods on the shelves. He saw Emmett Kelly statues, pennants, and posters. He bumped into his uncle when he stopped unexpectedly in front of the pharmacy. "Howdy, John. Need my usual." The man behind the counter, wearing a white coat, disappeared between the racks of shelves, which stored a vast array of medicines. He returned shortly with a small bottle of white pills for his uncle.

"What are those for?" Nick frowned, not knowing if he wanted to hear the answer.

"I've got high blood pressure and these pills help control it." Uncle Joe took a charge card from his wallet and paid for the medicine.

'Will it kill you?" Nick's mouth was dry and he had trouble forming the words to ask the question.

"Not if I take these pills and watch what I eat."

"Like cheeseburgers, fries and a shake?"

Uncle Joe took a long look at Nick, then leaned close to his ear and whispered, "Let's not tell Aunt Sara what we had for lunch. Our secret." He grabbed the pill bottle off the counter, tucked the credit card back into his wallet, and walked out of the store with Nick following in his footsteps.

Before chores, Nick showed his aunt all the goodies they had bought, plus he told her the exciting news about the scholarship. She said that she would stay close to the phone tomorrow afternoon waiting for the call from the college. "Oh, Nick. I do hope this works out for you. I wish you the best, dear." Neither Uncle Joe, nor Nick mentioned the high fat, high salt lunch.

After helping his uncle with evening chores, Nick tried the black halter on Elmer.

"He looks like a real gent. Don't he, *Yank*?"

Nick turned while tightening the neck strap and saw Rob standing by the gate with his hands behind his back. "Got your birthday present with me."

"You didn't need to get me any gift." Nick finished fastening the buckle, then smoothed down the fur on Elmer's neck. He looked mighty fine wearing the new leather halter.

"Told ya I had something special." From behind his back he pulled out a silver sword and with both hands presented it to Nick. "Do it proud, *Yank*. Do it proud."

CHAPTER THIRTEEN

 ICK TOSSED THE leather lead over Elmer's neck and walked to the gate, never once taking his eyes from the sword. "Where did you get that, Rob?" Nick was overwhelmed with confliction emotions.

"It's been in my family for years. Now it's yours."

Nick stared at the sword, glad to be separated from it by the gate. "I don't want it. Take it back. It belongs in your family."

Rob lowered his hands and sat down on a hay bale, resting the sword across his knees. "Before you decide, first, hear me out. Long ago, one of my kin, Nate McFarley, set out to find his brother, Rob, who had joined the Confederate Calvary. Ya see, Rob fought at Wilson Creek and was already dead, shot through the heart, when Nate found him." Rob had to pause for a moment before continuing. Both Nick and Elmer stood still listening to the tale.

"Well, Nate took his brother's sword and his horse. That mare sure was a beauty. She was a strawberry-roan. Anyways, he traveled home with a heavy heart only to learn that while he had been gone, his pa had been forced to fight for the Union and was killed in a battle. So, he arrived home to find that his ma was sick with a broken heart. The farm was a lost cause, so he took his ma to a neighbor and some say he joined Quantrill's gang and terrorized the countryside. That boy was filled with an anger burning within.

Nate rode that strawberry-roan with a vengeance, slicing down anything, or anyone in his path."

"Then one day, he rode into the yard of his neighbor to visit his ma, and he saw Becky hanging up the laundry in the backyard. His heart, which had been encased in ice, melted at the sight of her sweet face. But the country was fighting a war; it wasn't his place in time to fall in love. He slowly backed out of the yard and continued fighting for the South, but his heart wasn't in it any more. He had lost his passion for revenge and was just marking time till he might ask Becky for her hand."

Nick interrupted the narrative and said, "He does ask Becky to marry him, and she says yes. I know cause I saw it." Although Nick's statement sounded rather off the wall, Rob seemed to accept it.

"Well, yes. Nate does marry Becky, but it wasn't all peaches and cream for the two of them. Nate's ma died shortly after the war ended. Nate came home for good riding the strawberry-roan. His only possession, besides his horse, was the silver sword. After they were married, Becky and Nate worked mighty hard to fix up the old farm. Slowly, they turned it into a place to call home. Becky had two daughters before she died, poor thing."

"She dies? But he loved her." Nick folded his arms on the top boards of the pen and rested his chin on them.

"Sometimes your love can't stop death, but it can help you to carry on." Rob shook his head. "Enough with the old legends. Anyhow, all the kin is gone now. I place this sword and its history in your safe keeping."

"Thanks, Rob. I'll take good care of it." Nick now understood why Rob was giving him the sword and he felt proud to be worthy of the task.

Rob stood and placed the sword on a nearby bale of hay. He unlatched the gate and swung it wide. "Lead Elmer out here. Let's get working."

Together, Rob and Nick trimmed Elmer's long fur, they washed and brushed him till he shone and then walked him, on the lead, until it was too dark to see. Elmer stood still when asked and followed in Nick's footsteps without pulling.

"I think he's ready, *Yank*. He show's promise. Too bad I can't be there to watch you when you win the show."

"You're going, aren't you?" Nick walked Elmer back to his pen and put him away for the night.

"I can't. I have someplace else to be. You're a good man for a *Yankee*." Rob stuck his bony hand out to shake with Nick, then he turned and faded into the night.

Nick watched him leave. He had a feeling he wouldn't see him again, at least not in this lifetime. Nick walked over to the hay bale, where the sword rested and knelt beside it. He stared at the silver weapon and wondered about its bloody history. Finally, his eyes started to burn and he was forced to blink. He reached out his right arm and gingerly touched the sword with his fingers. He waited for his world to fade, or to become lightheaded, even dizzy, but nothing changed. He figured he had learned all that the sword needed to teach him. But he was wrong.

As he sat looking at the sword, a memory of one hot summer day that happened long ago came into his mind. It was of the day his dad had come home from work early and helped him learn to ride his bike down the sidewalk. His dad ran along Nick, who was peddling for all he was worth, ready to catch him if he started to fall.

Nick picked up the sword in his calloused hands, tears rolling down his cheeks. "I loved you, Dad. I wanted you to come home that night. I didn't want you to die. I need you now." As he cried he gripped the sharp blade tighter and sliced himself lightly across his palms. The pain cut into his sorrow, stemming the flow of his grief.

Slowly, his vision blurred and he saw the young soldier, Nate, standing over a freshly dug grave. Nick could see Becky's name chiseled into the stone grave marker. He heard Nate talking. "You took my heart and my hope for the future when you died Becky. But, you did leave me with something." Nate looked out across a field laden with ripe corn. He looked at a house so new the sap was still dripping from the rough-cut lumber. He looked at his two daughters, who were playing with their rag dolls, under the oak tree in the yard. Nate pulled back his shoulders and stood tall in his black leather boots. He turned away from the grave, leaving Becky's body in the ground, but wrapping the love they had shared tightly around his soul. He walked towards the dream Becky had left him, their two daughters.

As Nate faded from his sight, Nick picked up the sword and walked to the house. He had a show to win tomorrow and a dream of his own to fulfill.

CHAPTER FOURTEEN

 ICK WAS DRESSED and in the kitchen before the rooster had a chance to unruffled his feathers, stand on his toes and crow. He gulped a glass of milk and grabbed a bagel, coated in honey, from his aunt's outstretched hand.

"Happy Birthday, Nick." After handing him the bagel, she gave him a quick hug. Nick smiled at her, took a bite of the bagel, then hurried out to Elmer's pen. On the way, he quickly checked on Rose. She was still curled in a ball sleeping.

"Ready for the big day?" He quietly asked the bull as he picked up the brush, entered the pen, and began grooming him. The fur on the side the bull had slept on was flat and caked with dried manure. He worked until he heard his uncle bringing in the milking cows. He collected his brush, comb, and show halter, placing them on the seat of the yellow truck making sure he wouldn't forget them. He noticed the tan stock trailer had been connected to the hitch.

Milking seemed to take forever, as Nick was thinking more about showing Elmer than milking the cows. He was relieved when his uncle told him that he'd finish up with the milking and feeding the cows and calves. "You go and get ready. I hooked the trailer up for you. Your aunt and I will be there to watch you show Elmer. Look for us in the stands. Let Elmer strut his stuff, you'll be sure to win. Happy Birthday, Nick." Uncle Joe patted Nick on the back. Nick wished he felt as confident as his uncle did.

Before loading Elmer, Nick showered and pulled on the new black jeans with the silver rivets around the pockets. He carefully tucked in the dark-green western shirt with the eagle embroider across the yoke and then he tightened his belt. Sitting on the edge of his bed, he pulled on the black leather boots. Last but not least, he slipped his dad's broken pocket- watch into his back pocket for luck. On the way out the door, he kissed Aunt Sara on the check, waved goodbye, and backed the stock trailer close to the barn door. It took him six tries before he got close enough. He used Elmer's old halter to lead him into the trailer. He followed meekly, not giving Nick any trouble. He tied the bull on a short lead to a metal ring welded inside the trailer. He loaded a few flakes of hay and the water bucket. He was ready to roll.

Slowly, he drove down the drive and over to Amy's house. He had to wait a few minutes for her as he was running ahead of schedule. Elmer pawed at the floor and bellowed a few times impatient to be on his way.

"Hi, Nick." Amy opened the passenger door and slid beside him. "How's Elmer?"

"All spruced up and ready to show."

"You look mighty trim yourself." Amy's eyes worked over his fine form. "Happy Birthday." Amy handed him a tiny square box wrapped in purple foil.

"What's this?" Nick ripped off the wrapping paper and held a little white box in the palm of his hand. He opened the lid and saw a gold key chain with a brown and white plastic cow dangling from it.

"When I saw this, I thought it would be perfect for you to hang in your truck."

"Thanks, Amy." Nick unclasped the lock and hung the key chain securely onto the rear view mirror. The plastic cow seemed to enjoy the view as it swung freely in all directions.

The Little Honey Bee pulled the stock trailer smoothly, not troubled by the 2,000 pound bull riding inside. Nick drove onto the fair grounds and was directed over to the competitor's quarters by a man wearing orange gloves, and waving a cane with a yellow rag attached to the top.

Amy helped Nick unload and settle Elmer. They tied him to the outside of the trailer, filled his water bucket, and threw him a flake of hay.

Nick turned to Amy and said, "You keep an eye on him while I go regis-ter." Nick followed the signs to a white building, where a line had formed. After a half hour wait, he had acquired a white show number, that he was to attach to the back of his shirt, along with orders to be in the ring at 12:30 P.M. That was when the Jersey bulls were to be shown.

He had two hours to groom Elmer and wait. Amy and Nick took turns staying with the bull and walking around looking at all the competitors. Nick saw many different types of bulls tied up to trailers in the parking lot. He could identify the Brown Swiss, Holsteins, and Jerseys. There were a few breeds he had never seen before. Each breed competed in their own class, then the top bull in each class would compete against each other for the grand prize of 5,000 dollars. The competition would be stiff.

Nick watched the Holstein bull class perform, which was just before his. He watched closely and tried to pick up some pointers. The Jersey class was announced on time, and Nick led Elmer into the ring. The ring was covered in a deep layer of sawdust. Nick led Elmer on his left, keeping him towards the judge. There were seventeen other Jersey bulls, but Elmer was outstanding, and chosen to be the winner of the class. Nick had made it to the finals.

After the other classes had shown, the top bull of each class was asked to enter the ring. The judge watched closely as the owners led their bulls around him. The judge felt their thick coats and muscle tone. He checked their confirmation closely looking for any flaws in these fine animals.

Nick's shirt was stained under his arms and down his back with sweat. His arms were beginning to ache from holding Elmer on a short lead. On one of his passes around the ring he spied his aunt and uncle sitting by Amy in the stands. He nodded his head at them, but didn't dare wave.

Finally, the judge had made his decision. He asked Nick to lead his bull to the front of the line. Elmer pranced beside Nick to the designated spot. He was strutting his stuff, a natural show-off. Two other bulls, Fit to Show, the Brown Swiss, and Big Mac, the Holstein, were told to fall in line behind him. The other bulls were asked to leave.

The judge took a final walk around the top three bulls, stopping in front of Elmer. Nick found himself holding his breath and forcing back a smile. His heart was pounding in his chest. The judge turned and began to walk to the official table at the side of the ring to announce his decision, when he dropped the clipboard that he was carrying. He bent over, and exposed his rear to Elmer. Elmer saw the target, pawed once, lowered his head and charged. He ripped the leather lead out of Nick's hands and bucked his massive head right in to the judge's behind, sending him sprawling head first into the sawdust of the show ring.

A hush fell over the crowd, as they waited to see if the judge was going to be okay. Nick ran forward and yanked on Elmer's lead, pulling him away from the fallen judge. Several paramedics, who were on hand for the show, rushed over to check out the judge.

The judge rose slowly and stumbled to his feet. A loud applause from the crowd voiced their concern for his well being. Several helpful hands wiped down his pants and shirt in an attempt to dislodge the clinging sawdust. The judge coughed a few times and shook his head. He signaled to the paramedics to move out of the ring, refusing any more help. He insisted that he was fine. One of the paramedics handed him back his clipboard on his way out of the ring. The judge walked rather stiffly to the microphone. Nick led Elmer back into line. Nick's face was red with embarrassment and he couldn't look the judge in the eye.

"Attention, please. I will announce the first place winner, but first, I'm sorry to say that, Elmer of Sunny Hill Dairy is disqualified due to unruly behavior. Young man you are asked to leave with your bull."

Nick lowered his head, totally embarrassed. He felt like he was walking on two wooden legs as he led Elmer across the ring. His throat was dry, but he couldn't summon up enough spit to swallow. Elmer proudly pranced beside him as they left the ring, not understanding that he was leaving in disgrace, not a winner. The crowd was silent, agreeing with the judge's decision. Amy, Uncle Joe, and Aunt Sara stood and made their way out of the stands.

Once outside the ring, Nick clenched his teeth to prevent himself from crying out with frustration and disappointment. He concentrated on walking Elmer briskly back to the yellow truck. "Elmer, you stupid bull. I've lost everything. Uncle Joe should have shot you a year ago. You're worthless." He jerked hard on the lead shank trying to cause Elmer pain. But Elmer couldn't understand Nick's anger, didn't they just win?

Back at the trailer Nick took off the black leather show halter and tied Elmer up using the old one. As Nick tossed the new halter through the open truck window, his eyes noticed a rusty pocketknife sitting on the truck seat. A piece of white paper was tucked underneath. Nick stopped and took a second look, not believing what he thought he saw. But, there it was, a rusty pocketknife, stamped with a C, and covered with green slime.

CHAPTER FIFTEEN

 HE FIRST THING Nick thought was that Rob had come after all. He stepped away from the truck and look around in all directions, but didn't see his friend. He walked back over to the truck and opened the passenger door. Without touching the rusty knife, he slipped the white paper out from underneath. He unfolded the note and read:

> Bad things happen to good people. It's all in the way that you react to the events that makes the outcome either a blessing or a curse.

Nick read the message several times. The words made him stop and think about how he had reacted over losing the prize money. He was mad at Elmer because of the prank he had pulled, but wasn't it his own fault for not breaking him of it? And were his dreams really lost? He thought of his Aunt Sara and Uncle Joe, and the job opportunity they had offered him. His uncle had even said that he could borrow *The Little Honey Bee* to drive back and forth to college. With the money his uncle paid him to milk cows and help on the farm, he would still be able to afford at least one course this semester, no matter what. He'd just have to work harder to achieve his goals. The more he thought about it, the better he felt.

Nick tucked the note into his pocket, his fingers coming in contact with his dad's broken watch. "I'm not going to give up, Dad. I'll still make you proud of me."

"Nick. Are you okay?" Amy reached Nick just steps ahead of his aunt and uncle.

"Yeah. It's my fault I didn't work with Elmer more. I should have broken him of that bad habit. He could have won Uncle Joe, I'm sorry."

"Tough break, son. Elmer can't resist a target." Uncle Joe was disappointed with Nick being disqualified. He knew Elmer was the rightful winner of that class.

Amy had taken hold of Nick's hand, and was stroking his arm tenderly. Somehow, her touch took away some of the sting of losing.

Uncle Joe filled Nick in with the results of the show. "I heard that Big Mack of Runningwell Dairy won with his Holstein bull. He's not near as nice as Elmer. You should have won."

Aunt Sara came and stood by Nick's side. "I've got some wonderful news for you Nick, dear. I think that you could use some about now. Martha from the college called before we left. She said that you've been approved for a RMI scholarship. Is that good news, dear?"

"I've been approved? That's great news!" Nick turned towards his uncle. "Can I borrow the truck to drive to college this fall, Uncle Joe?"

"Of course, son, of course you can." Uncle Joe was happy to hear that Nick wanted to use the yellow truck and that he had plans to be there in the fall.

"Hello, everyone." Mr. Peebles of Milkyway Dairy walked up to the little group. "That's a mighty fine sire you've got there. I'd like to breed twenty of my top cows to him, you interested?"

Nick looked to his uncle for the answer and was surprised by the response.

"That's up to you, Nick. Elmer's your responsibility from now on."

Nick turned to answer Mr. Peebles. "That would be fantastic, but do you still want to breed him after that stunt he pulled back in the ring?"

"I'm not breeding for personality, son. He's a fine bull and will improve my milk production." Mr. Peebles shook hands with Nick. "I came to talk with you the other day, but you were test driving Bobbie's truck. I've got five heifers for sale. Are you interested in buying them?" He looked at Nick and waited for an answer.

"I didn't win the prize money, sir. I can't afford to buy them now." Nick looked down at the beaten grass around the trailer, still feeling embarrassed about the bull's antics.

"I'm asking 1,250 dollars a head. As they freshen you can pay me out of your milk check plus 9% interest on the outstanding balance."

"You'd do that for me?" Nick jerked his head up and looked at Mr. Peebles to see if he was serious.

"It's a business deal, not a favor. It works for both of us. What do you say?" Mr. Peebles stuck out his hand. Nick grabbed it and sealed the deal with a firm shake. "Welcome to the dairy business, kid. I'll bring the heifers over in the morning and take the bull back to my place. You decide a fair price." Mr. Peebles turned to Joe. "That's a good kid there. He'll go far." Mr. Peebles patted Uncle Joe on the back and walked away.

"Elmer's going to be a daddy!" Nick smiled and looked over at Elmer who was picking at the flake of hay.

Uncle Joe couldn't help laughing. "He's already a daddy. He's Rose's sire." Uncle Joe informed Nick who looked at him with his mouth open. "He's bred almost all the cows on the place for the last year. He's a working boy. And who knows, thanks to your showing him, it looks like he'll even make us some money." Uncle Joe was quite proud of all three of his boys, Bobbie for his choice of bloodlines, Nick for taking his responsibilities seriously, and Elmer for being a fine bull. "Glad you bought those heifers, Nick. You made the right choice."

"Cake and ice cream back at the house, if anyone's interested?" Aunt Sara announced.

Nick, with the help of Amy, loaded Elmer, taking care to tie him tight so he wouldn't hurt himself. Amy climbed into the truck without seeing the rusty, green-covered pocketknife. As she sat on the seat, the knife slid down between the two cushions. In all the excitement, Nick had forgotten about it, and probably would for some time.

After the cake and ice cream was eaten, Nick drove Amy home thanking her for her help and for the key chain with the plastic cow. She promised to come over soon with her horse, Princess, and take him riding.

Nick had a personal interest in the cows now. Soon five of his would join the herd. He would keep a close eye on all the newborns and look for a little piece of Elmer in each and every one.   When Nick chose his four college classes for the fall semester, he chose only one computer course. The other three classes were farm related.

Nick hung the silver sword next to the dresser in his room. Every morning, after the rooster crowed, it was the first thing he saw. It was also the last thing he saw at night before he turned off the light, but not the last thing he touched. That would be his dad's broken pocket-watch.